I0654374

A NOVEL

LOVE
—— YOUR ——
ENEMIES

GRACE E. M. ALLAN

LOVE YOUR ENEMIES
Copyright © 2024 by Grace E.M. Allan

Scripture quotations are from the ESV® Bible (The Holy Bible, English Standard Version®), © 2001 by Crossway, a publishing ministry of Good News Publishers. Used by permission. All rights reserved. The ESV text may not be quoted in any publication made available to the public by a Creative Commons license. The ESV may not be translated in whole or in part into any other language. Scripture quotations taken from the Amplified® Bible (AMP), Copyright © 2015 by The Lockman Foundation. Used by permission. lockman.org. Used by permission. All rights reserved. Scripture quotations marked (TPT) are from The Passion Translation®. Copyright © 2017, 2018, 2020 by Passion & Fire Ministries, Inc. Used by permission. All rights reserved. ThePassionTranslation.com.

This is a work of fiction. Names, characters, places and incidents either are the product of the author's imagination or are used fictitiously, and any resemblance to actual persons, living or dead, businesses, companies, events, or locales is entirely coincidental.

ISBN: 978-1-4866-2515-4
eBook ISBN: 978-1-4866-2516-1

Word Alive Press
119 De Baets Street Winnipeg, MB R2J 3R9
www.wordalivepress.ca

WORD ALIVE
—P R E S S—

Cataloguing in Publication information can be obtained from Library and Archives Canada.

To Jesus Christ, the Son of God,
who died in the place of all mankind.
My life belongs to you.

To family and the community of Christ followers
who have inspired this book.

You have heard that it was said, "You shall love your neighbor and hate your enemy." But I say to you, Love your enemies and pray for those who persecute you, so that you may be sons of your Father who is in heaven. (Matthew 5:43–45, ESV)

The thief comes only to steal and kill and destroy. I came that they may have life and have it abundantly. (John 10:10, ESV)

I will instruct you and teach you in the way you should go; I will counsel you with my eye upon you. (Psalm 32:8, ESV)

CONTENTS

ACKNOWLEDGEMENTS

Many dear ones in Christ have been part of this journey, their real-life stories, hearts, and characters having contributed to the book. These treasured brothers and sisters in Christ have contributed to the storytelling through living their lives.

To my parents and sister, for the love of God that is evident through their lives.

I must also thank the leaders of Youth with a Mission, who have helped me understand and personally experience God's heart as Father Light.

Thank you, Jerry Baxter and Jarkko Ketola, for sharing your personal testimonies and contributing to this novel storytelling.

As for the worldwide body of Christ, we are members of one body. Jesus is the chief cornerstone, the author and perfector of our faith.

I also thank Matt Tommey and the Created to Thrive community for their encouragement to step out in faith and creativity.

Thank you to the whole team at Word Alive Press for their part in editing, printing and publishing this book.

Thank you to the whole team at Word Alive Press for their part in editing, printing and publishing this book.

Finally, the Holy Spirit inspired and led me throughout the writing of this book. And I must acknowledge that God's character, vision, and thoughts are not our thoughts, nor are his ways our ways.

DEAR READER

Welcome! It is humbling to know that this story has the potential to influence your mind, heart, and journey, depending on your choice of response. Nonetheless, I hope it will help you better understand what's going on in the world today and the spiritual influences behind it.

Quite recently, during the editing process of this book, I spent an hour in conversation with a seventy-five-year-old blind man on his birthday. During the course of a one-hour flight, we talked of many things regarding life, God, religion, faith, and spirituality. We listened to one another with open minds and a willingness to learn.

One of the things I learned from this man is that we all have so much more in common than what divides us. Over the last few years, since 2019, there has been more division, hurtful words, and broken relationships than ever before. Violence, hatred, chaos, anxiety, war, arguments, and anger are all on the rise. None of us are guiltless and all have fallen short.

Yet these things are evidence to me of our desperate need of a different narrative, one based on redemption, rescue, hope, and truth.

This book is a combination of allegory and real life. It expresses many joyful and painful moments that reflect the truth. Figuratively speaking, it's like a table, with many people present—and a spot is open for you, dear reader. You are welcome to gather with us around the table, and at this table the story is told by the lives of those seated around it.

This novel has a lot of intense moments, but I want to share some things upfront. Although this book is about Christianity and the God of the Bible, elements of fiction are used to illustrate key points, particularly the talk around rival family members, initiations, goals, and rings. There is also a great deal of violence, prayer, emotions, and the miraculous. This is not included to deny reality but to help you encounter God personally.

In the midst of this novel are a series of photographs; a study the process for caterpillars to become a butterfly. This journey can in a way, reflect the hope of God's transforming love in our lives; the kind of love that is willing to die for one's enemies. These photos of creation can speak more than a thousand words to you.

In the midst of this novel are a series of photographs; a study the process for caterpillars to become a butterfly. This journey can in a way, reflect the hope of God's transforming love in our lives; the kind of love that is willing to die for one's enemies. These photos of creation can speak more than a thousand words to you.

Storytelling is a tool and can aid a reader in their journey of Christian faith. That being said, I encourage you to actively pursue Yahweh, who has proven his love for humanity—for while we were sinners, Christ died for us.

Other aspects of the story are based on the real-life stories of people I know personally, as well as experiences that have been shared with me. Many people in my community have aided in inspiring this novel. Other aspects are imagined depictions of what might be possible.

A friend last year shared the following thoughts: "When we look around, we get frustrated. When we look within, we get discouraged. When we look to the Lord, we are transformed." The purpose of this story is to bring glory to God. It has also been written in the hope that your faith will be directed not at man or created things but the Creator who made all things.

God bless your reading!

PROLOGUE

In a time and place beyond our understanding, something extraordinary occurred. The God who created the universe decided to take on the form of a human being, born into a poor family as a baby. He came on a mission from his heavenly Father, which meant experiencing all the ups and downs of life.

Despite being misunderstood and rejected, he continued on his mission. Even when his closest friends betrayed and denied him, he forgave them, along with those who put him to death. He was beaten, tortured, and buried.

But on the third day, he returned to life, making it possible for God's light to be seen in dark circumstances. The mighty power of God rose him from the dead and seated him high above all names.

ONE

The throne room of heaven radiated pure joy. The light filling the space wasn't a mere flicker but a constant, dazzling brilliance that illuminated every corner. There were no shadows, no darkness to dampen the spirits of those who resided there. The colours were so vivid that they made the very earth seem dull and lifeless by comparison.

A humble warrior angel conversed with the one who sat on the throne, the one whose name was above all others.

The angel longed to understand the mighty one's plan of salvation and perplexing thoughts on humanity.

"Mighty Lord, why did you create humans?" the angel inquired. "Why do you care for them so deeply?"

Father Light, sitting next to Lord Yeshua, answered with love and kindness. "My mighty warrior, we created humans out of love and for love. We wanted to give them a place to live, to believe, and to know us as family. Every day we give them a chance to turn to us and accept our love. When we welcome someone to heaven, we ask only one question: 'Did you love as we loved you?' We have dreamed of each person since before time began, of the adventures and lives we would share. It breaks our hearts when even one person fails to discover the depth of love they were created for. Without our love, fear, anxiety, and hate grow. But perfect love casts out fear. Sadly, many souls are destroyed by pride and self-determination. Out of perfect love, we give them the choice to determine what defines them, how they will live on the earth, and where they will live in eternity."

A messenger arrived with news of man named Aaron who was about to enter a coffee shop named Sailors cove in Sunny-side Beach. Father Light observed Aaron's heart and knew of his wickedness and the evil he'd done. Yet Father Light chose to have mercy on him. He watched as Aaron entered one of the most dangerous parts in the city.

"Why do people strive to fit in when they were born to shine with their own unique light, honouring the ones who gave them life?" Lord Yeshua wondered aloud.

Aaron had been entrusted with a critical mission by his family: to obtain a powerful weapon to help them achieve their ultimate goal of vanquishing their long-standing rival clan. He took great pride in having been chosen for this task and dressing in attire that would blend in with the locals.

As he ventured through the grimy alleyways of the slums, Aaron found Gruff, his former comrade-in-arms from the army. Aaron exchanged a hefty amount of American currency for a small brown bottle of bitter heart poison which he had been sent to retrieve for his family's use in their war against their enemies back home in Canada.

Both men sported iron-engraved signet rings on their left hand ring fingers. They served as a symbol of their unwavering allegiance and loyalty to their family's cause.

With swift movements, they slid back hidden compartments, revealing small pins which they then used to administer to themselves a dose of the same poison. The sensation that engulfed their bodies was nothing short of exhilarating. It fuelled their hatred for their rivals and boosted their confidence in the coming showdown.

To these plans of overthrowing them, the mighty ones on the thrones laughed.

In contrast to the leaders of Aaron's family, known for their cruel and destructive ways, the rival family was known for an unwavering commitment to love and compassion. They believed that everyone deserved to be treated with respect, love, and kindness. Yet all of creation was accountable to them whose thrones were founded on integrity, wisdom, truth, and justice.

The Father, Son, and Holy Spirit were the heads of this rival family. They understood that those who opposed them had been led to believe that they were weak and powerless. Such people lived in a state of bondage disguised as freedom, unable to see the truth.

Unknown to Aaron, the values of the rival family had been ingrained in him from his conception in his mother's womb. They had lain dormant, like seeds buried deep within the earth, waiting for the right circumstances to awaken. Soon enough, those deeply planted seeds would begin to sprout.

For the past few days, Aaron had been staying in a seedy motel near the slums. He knew he would have to leave the area as soon as possible with the vial he had acquired. It was crucial to keep the contents of the vial secret, as it was highly valuable and could attract unwanted attention.

With a heavy heart, he retrieved his bag from the rented locker in a busy bus depot. The depot bustled with people waiting for transportation. The noise was deafening.

Knowing he had to be careful with the vial, Aaron went into a bathroom stall and unscrewed the top of his electric shaver. He carefully placed the vial inside the hidden compartment there and packed cotton balls around it to keep it safe.

Once he was satisfied that the vial was secure, he restowed the shaver in his bag. The only other person to know the vial's true value was his dark master, the same master who had advised him to check his backpack on the way back to Canada, to prevent security from discovering it.

As Aaron left the depot and made his way out of the slums on foot, he couldn't help but feel a sense of relief. Now that he had successfully acquired the vial, he could return to the northern hemisphere. He caught a taxi to the airport and checked in for his flight. Soon he had boarded the plane, all the while wondering what the future held for him.

From his first-class seat, he embarked on the long flight to New York where he planned to enjoy the latest Broadway shows. Then, after three days of extravagance, he would return to Canada.

As he watched the scenery pass below him, his thoughts drifted to his childhood. He remembered what life had been like in the palace growing up. His father had often been distant, spending much of his time working as a spy for wealthy businessmen. Nevertheless, he had admired his father, looking up to him as a hero and aspiring to be like him.

Aaron had grown up without knowing who his father worked for, but he now had a burning desire to become the best. While devoting himself to his studies, he had realized his own remarkable ability to remember facts and solve complex problems. IQ tests recognized his intelligence as well and had hailed him as having a brilliant mind.

After graduating high school, Aaron had joined the army while attending university. He'd trained to become a sniper, performing with flying colours. He had become a true asset to his team in the military, saving their lives on more than one occasion. In return, they had protected him with fierce loyalty, creating a bond that made them closer than comrades-in-arms; they were brothers, united by their shared experiences.

Throughout this period of his life, Aaron had discovered his purpose in serving his master, a powerful and dark figure who revealed who his father had truly been working for all those years. Aaron's life was no longer his own. He had given it away.

In the meantime, the rival family had kept a close eye on Aaron, trying to stir his emotions through the Holy Spirit. They had long hoped to awaken in him a desire for a different way of life.

Daydreaming his way through the flight, Aaron couldn't help but think about his upcoming date with Claudia. They had met while on assignment in Oak Creek, where she'd worked as a waitress. Aaron had convinced her to leave everything behind and come with him to New York.

Just six months later, though, he was already bored with her.

Lost in thought, Aaron received a message from his boss, instructing him to break Claudia's heart. The twisted idea brought a wicked smile to his face.

TWO

U pon his arrival in New York, Aaron checked into his luxurious penthouse suite. He quickly dressed in a tuxedo and
made his way to Broadway. He had reserved a box for the past
fourteen seasons in this theatre and was excited to attend once
again. The red carpet and chairs fit his style much more appro-
priately than the slums he had been in just a few hours before.

His companion, Claudia, soon joined him in the box. Aaron intended to give her one final payout before they parted
ways.

After the ballet, the couple went to an upscale restaurant.
That's where Aaron informed Claudia that their relationship was
over. He handed her a leather bag containing rare gold coins.

Devastated, she had believed he loved her unconditionally
and had seen her inner beauty. Now she realized he had only
been interested in using her. Her heart shattered into a million
pieces as she came to terms with the truth.

Devoid of empathy, Aaron took pleasure in Claudia's pain,
echoing the wickedness of his dark master.

As Claudia finished her meal and got up to leave, Aaron
discreetly settled the bill and arranged for a ride home.

Little did he know that the heads of the rival family had been keeping a watchful eye on him, studying his every move. They were preparing to approach him with a surprising invitation he could not have anticipated.

On the way home, the taxi driver turned the radio to a station playing some absurd song he had never heard of before. The band was called For King and Country.

Aaron took out a $50 bill. "This is yours if you change the music to the classical station." He enjoyed the soothing sound of strings and opera.

"No way, man," said the driver. "This is a song everyone needs to hear!"

The man hummed along and even moved his hand to turn up the volume. As he did so, Aaron noticed his gold signet ring, displaying the crest of the rival family. It shimmered in the dim light and Aaron pocketed the money.

As the song continued to play, anger simmered in Aaron's heart. He studied the odometer, though, and suddenly had an idea. He took out the vial he'd retrieved in Argentina, along with a wad of ones and fives. He drizzled some of the poison onto the paper, his black gloves preventing the poison from affecting him.

"I'm not putting up with this crap," Aaron ordered when he'd finished his silent work. "Pull over!"

The driver put on his blinker and found a safe place to park. Aaron gave the driver the poisoned cash, then got out of the car and walked away. As he went looking for another ride, the song's chords faded away in the wind.

Faintly, though, the strange lyrics resonated deep within him. But he was blood-bound to his master.

Aaron had a pleasant morning after spending the night with two expensive call girls. He felt content and satisfied as he ordered a substantial breakfast rich in aroma and flavours, consisting of bacon, eggs, toast, pancakes, juice, and coffee. He savoured every bite.

After breakfast, he lounged around and read his current science book, sipping coffee and enjoying the peace and quiet. Feeling energized, he decided to hit the private gym downstairs dressed in comfortable sweatpants and a clean T-shirt.

Upon reaching the gym, he noticed a well-built man with long, beautiful dreads wearing earbuds. Aaron assumed that the other man wasn't interested in conversation, which was perfectly fine with him. But a few minutes later, the man exited his machine, pulled out his earbuds, and approached Aaron.

"Hey man, can I tell you something?" the stranger asked.

Initially pleased to have the company, Aaron became less enthusiastic when he saw the man's T-shirt. It read "Lifestyle Christianity" underneath the logo of a red lion. He felt annoyed.

Aaron decided to end the conversation before it began.

"If I say yes, will you leave me alone?"

But the stranger was persistent. "I'd say yes, but I can't… because I'm compelled to ask: do you know how much the head of my family, the God who made all things, loves you?"

Aaron was taken aback by the stranger's question. Without thinking, he kicked him in the eye with his left foot, followed by a punch in the gut that doubled him over.

Then, without a backward glance, Aaron walked out of the gym, leaving the stranger behind.

Aaron had a dream the following morning, after a night of partying. Everything was dark and he found himself lying on the floor, paralyzed. Mouth dry. Skin covered with sores and burning with pain. From far off, he heard sneering laughter and knew he'd missed an opportunity of the ages.

A snarling voice hissed into his ear. "You belong to me forever and will never leave this place!"

Aaron forced himself awake with a gasp. He was covered in sweat and the sheets stuck to his skin. He hopped out of bed and into the shower, chilly and shaking from his night vision.

"This is your life and purpose," the master's voice whispered in his ear. "You are mine."

Aaron could not deny it, for this was his chosen life.

He sat on the leather couch and turned on the television. The news anchor was reporting on a hit-and-run robbery on the strip where he'd been the night before. A woman was in the hospital with life-threatening injuries.

"The woman is fighting for her life in a hospital ICU," the anchor said. "She was found wearing a torn and bloodied ball gown, like a real-life princess. The question everyone is asking is simple: where is her prince?"

Aaron felt a foreign feeling—guilt. He squirmed in his seat to alleviate the sinking feeling in his gut.

The anchor continued by replaying the police's request that anyone with information on the woman's identity come forward.

Aaron recognized the unconscious, beaten woman in the photograph. It was Claudia. Some part of him felt horrified that he had contributed to what had happened to her.

"Her blood is on your hands," said his dark master.

The guilt pricked his conscience and he pulled out an untraceable phone with a voice changer to call the police department's hotline. Even as the phone rang, he wondered why he was doing it.

Torn up inside, he told the operator what he knew: what Claudia had on her at the time of her assault, her full name, her hometown, and her parents' address.

Afterward he promptly hung up and removed the phone's battery. He wiped both and flushed them down the toilet.

Hurriedly, he packed his bag and left for the airport. Upon arrival, he could change his flight without question to the next available route home. He needed to get back home.

THREE

In the following months, Aaron was given various opportunities to create conflict and animosity between members of the rival family. Thanks to the potent poison he had obtained in South America, his master was able to delight in the destruction of their rival family. In return, Aaron was rewarded with immense wealth.

Despite his success, a part of him grew deeply disturbed by the life he was living, though he felt powerless to change it. The poison Aaron had brought back was designed to bring out the dark and selfish desires of those who consumed it, causing internal division in the family of light. Once exposed, family members would begin to fight amongst themselves, driven by their greedy desires instead of treating one another as equals and with respect.

The values of Aaron's dark master were vastly different from those of Father Light. While Father Light loved and cherished each member of his family uniquely and sought to restore them to their true potential, Aaron's family had a sinister agenda. They aimed to make the children of their rivals forget their identity, purpose, and origin.

Aaron's dark master had urged him to buy a luxurious waterfront condo in Sunny-side Beach, Ontario. He had gone on fifty-two dates with women in just eight months, making frequent trips to New York throughout that time to attend shows, parties, and concerts. Aaron often visited local coffee shops where he charmed vulnerable women, worming his way into their hearts and leaving them broken.

On a warm summer day, Aaron walked into a cozy coffee shop called The Sailor's Cove. The shop usually had a lively atmosphere, filled with the soothing aroma of locally baked sweets and freshly ground coffee. But on this particular day, he witnessed an unexpected and astonishing scene. The room was filled with radiant light and a woman was running and dancing around, shouting for joy.

"I'm healed! I'm healed!"

To Aaron's surprise, he noticed an empty wheelchair behind the woman, and a man stood nearby with a broad grin on his face. It was evident that something miraculous had happened here, for the woman was no longer bound by her wheelchair. The atmosphere was electric and everyone seemed to be in a state of wonder at what had taken place.

Aaron felt confused and overwhelmed by the unusual and powerful light. It seemed to be emanating from the woman. He turned and ran out the door as fast as he could, feeling as if his life depended on it.

Despite no one chasing him, he continued to run until he was more than a block from the coffee shop.

The heads of the rival family watched as Aaron ran away. Power radiated from them in vibrant colours and blinding light. Their mighty servants sang of God's purity and holiness. The world needed to witness the truth about these ancient families that warred against each other. It was time for a mighty revelation about the meaning and origin of life.

The Holy Trio—Father Light, his Son Yeshua, and the Holy Spirit—provided for undeserved mercy and forgiveness cover the earth, but those who refused to accept their gift of love would face death.

As Aaron trudged on, his stomach growled and gnawed at him, but it was the hunger within that caused the real discomfort. His mind was in turmoil, his steps faltering as he tried to make sense of what he had just witnessed. How could a paralyzed woman suddenly walk again? What kind of power could make that happen?

These questions raced through his mind, each more confusing than the last. Doubt crept in as he wondered whether he had been wrong in placing his allegiance with his dark master. Was there a force more potent, one he was unaware of?

The need for answers consumed him, but he had no idea where to turn.

As he strolled along a quiet residential street, Aaron suddenly realized that he had no idea where he was. He tried to retrace his steps and find his way back to the main road, but every turn seemed to lead him deeper into unfamiliar territory. His headache intensified, throbbing in time with his footsteps. His anxiety and fear grew and he felt lost and out of control, filled with a deep sense of desperation that threatened to burst out at any moment.

In the midst of this torment, Aaron's dark master relished his suffering.

As the weight of his struggles became too much to bear, a deep need awakened within in, urging him to release his anguish into the universe.

"Help me, God!" he cried out with all his might, hoping that some divine force would hear his plea and ease his pain.

From a distance, Aaron noticed a man cycling along the sidewalk ahead of him. As the cyclist came closer, Aaron noticed that he had sandy brown hair that curled underneath his helmet. He had a backpack on and wore a soccer jersey, black shorts, mismatched socks, sport sunglasses, and worn tennis shoes.

The man pulled over and stopped alongside Aaron.

"Hey man," he said in a deep baritone, lowering his glasses. His accent was unmistakably Australian. "Did you just ask God for help?"

Aaron was feeling embarrassed and decided to tell a lie. "No, I didn't."

"Do you need help with something?"

Aaron felt the flush of shame spread across his face and down to his heart. He swallowed hard and forced himself to admit the truth.

"I'm sorry. I'm lost. I don't know where we are…"

It was a bitter pill to swallow for someone who had always prided himself on his independence. He couldn't help but feel a surge of self-loathing.

"It's perfectly fine to admit when you're feeling disoriented or uncertain of your whereabouts," said the cyclist. "If you'd like, I can assist you in finding your way to Crunchy Road. That's the primary street that leads to the waterfront. It's easily recognizable."

Aaron breathed a sigh of relief, though a tinge of embarrassment lingered in the pit of his stomach.

"Okay, let's go then," he said while turning around to walk alongside the stranger.

The sleek road bike rolled smoothly between them, its tires whispering against the pavement. The air was thick with the sweet scent of blooming flowers. The sound of birdsong filled the tranquil morning air.

"Just to clarify, my name is Ethan," the man said.

"Nice to meet you. I'm Aaron."

Ethan's calming presence seemed to radiate peace. It grounded Aaron and helped settle his emotions.

"Where are you headed?" Aaron asked, wanting to shift his focus from his feelings.

"The soccer field on Warrior Way, across Crunchy Road at the traffic lights. A bus stops there that will take me across town."

With no pressing engagements, and feeling curious, Aaron found himself intrigued about his new acquaintance.

"I couldn't help but notice your passion for soccer," Aaron said. "How long have you been playing?"

"As a young child, I was completely mesmerized it. My dad noticed my passion for the game and became my mentor, teaching me the basics. I was thrilled to learn as much as I could and quickly became immersed in the sport. My love for it grew stronger with each passing day. Soon it became more than just a hobby… it became a way of life. Do you share the same passion?"

"It's been a while, but I love staying active and playing sports."

"Would you like to join a group of us for a recreational game of soccer, Aaron?"

The question made Aaron feel slightly anxious and he wondered whether his master would approve.

"Perhaps," Aaron replied hesitantly. "How many people will be there?"

"Depends who's available. The maximum number is around fifteen, but we can play with fewer. It's essential to work on improving your skills and physical fitness to get better."

Aaron nodded. "What do you enjoy most about playing soccer compared to watching it on TV?"

Ethan took a pause. "Playing is much more exciting and engaging. When I'm on the field, I feel alive… facing the challenges, experiencing the joys, the humour, the teamwork, and everything that comes with it. It builds a sense of community between people. It's just awesome."

When the two men arrived at the corner of Crunchy Road, Aaron noticed the streetlight and bus stop nearby.

Ethan gestured towards the left. "That way leads to the waterfront district. The other way will take you to a shopping area and some more homes. But do you want to come with me to the soccer field across the street?"

Aaron was surprised by his own response. "Yeah, I think I'll join you and play for a while."

"Great!"

The two men crossed the street and soon reached the field where a third man was waiting for them by the soccer net, his bike parked next to him. He had a head of thick, curly brown hair that cascaded down his shoulders. Aaron couldn't help but feel like he'd seen the man somewhere before, but he couldn't quite place him.

"Hey Aaron, this is Trent," said the cyclist, making introductions.

Trent stepped forward and extended his hand. "Pleasure to meet you, Aaron." His smile was warm and welcoming. Trent spoke with a strong Scottish accent, and it made Aaron wonder if the man ever wore a kilt. "I heard Josh is on his way, and maybe Arden and a few others. Are you here to join us for a game?"

"Yes, I am."

"Awesome! Have you played before?"

"Yeah, but it's been a while."

"No worries! Our main goal is to have fun, learn, and do our best," Trent said. "We love to have a good laugh and share some jokes. Besides, our group consists of people with different skill levels. We've got some talented players, sure. Josh has coached soccer some, and a few others come from Brazil where they got really good as kids on the schoolyard. We all have distinct styles and strategies."

Trent placed a hand on Aaron's shoulder.

"Ethan's got an amazing one-touch kick." Trent smiled teasingly. "His moves are so graceful, he's almost like a ballerina!"

Ethan blushed. "Well, Trent's got a powerhouse kick himself. He can get the ball in from three-quarters of the way down the field with accuracy about seventy percent of the time..."

All three men laughed heartily.

"Want to see who wins today in the usual seven-minute match?" Trent asked. "Will it be graceful movements or powerhouse strength?"

Ethan broke out into a big smile. "Sure, let's get started!"

FOUR

Tina rode her bike with joy and enthusiasm along the quiet residential street, having tucked her amber-coloured hair into a loose ponytail underneath her helmet. Her green eyes and sunglasses sparkled in the summer sun. The warm weather, smell of blossoms, and sweet birdsong delighted her. She took a deep breath of the wind blowing gently off the lake.

As she rode, she heard laughter and recognized the voices of her friends, gathered at the soccer field at the end of the street. Tina parked her bike behind the restrooms, where it wouldn't be seen.

She walked towards them, spotting Trent right away. He was like a big brother to her. And there was Josh, a soccer coach who also mentored troubled teens. Next she recognized Arden, who worked at a local gym.

Her sister and a few other women would be arriving soon, but first she wanted to listen to the men unnoticed. While she was still single, she had the made the choice not to be alone with any group of men.

She put her backpack down on the grass and listened. That's when she detected an unfamiliar voice in the mix. She saw the new guy and heard Trent refer to him as Aaron. The newcomer kicked a soccer ball at the net and missed.

"Good try!" Trent shouted.

The sound of their laughter brought a smile to Tina's face. She felt grateful for each of her friends.

She brought her eyes up and watched as the men dragged a portable cloth circle onto the grass. Tina winced; in addition to grass, some dirt, and the occasional pebble, the local geese had been using this field as their personal washroom.

Trent and Ethan lined up, facing each other with the ball placed behind them. In the meantime, Josh had arrived and was reviewing the rules for the newcomer. The objective was for one player to kick the ball out of the designated circle, beyond the reach of his opponent. The mini-game would last precisely seven minutes, during which time the players would attempt to score as many times as possible as the clock continued to tick.

There were a few other rules as well. The players were only permitted to remove their footwear and exit the circle for fifteen seconds or less. Any shots made to sensitive body parts would lead to immediate disqualification of the player who'd made the shot. And if a player was pushed out of the ring, they would have to wait for three seconds before being allowed to re-enter the circle. During this brief delay, the other player would have an opportunity to kick the ball out of the circle and score a point, depending on where the ball was.

From the shadows, Tina watched Josh act as timekeeper.

"Three, two, one… go!" he called.

Ethan immediately dropped to the ground, crawled through Trent's legs, and scrambled towards the ball. He punched it out of the circle with his fist.

"Is that allowed?" the newcomer asked.

Josh shrugged his shoulders, his wavy brown hair moving with the wind. "There's no rule against it. One point for Ethan!"

Trent ran to get his soccer ball back into position. He faced Ethan again with a big grin on his face. His face seemed to radiate joy.

"Smart move, Ethan! But are you ready to hit the dirt?"

Trent faked left and went right, twisting around Ethan and giving the ball a powerful kick. His foot made contact with Ethan's shin guard, though, causing Ethan to trip and fall into the grass.

Trent kicked the ball out and returned to Ethan, offering him a hand up. Ethan took it and got back onto his feet.

The two players engaged in an intense mini-game, each trying to outdo the other. Ethan was quick on his feet, darting around the circle while Trent attempted to block his every move. They seemed evenly matched, with both men keeping pace.

In the last few seconds of the game, the score was tied at seven—until Trent made a daring move and tackled Ethan to the ground. He grabbed the ball and threw it out of the circle just as the timer went off.

Josh complimented the two on their skills and then the men reset.

After two more rounds, they all took a break. That's when Tina turned her head at the sound of her sister Ashley's car approaching. The car's muffler had fallen off and could be heard from several blocks away.

Just like the muffler, Tina could see and hear indicators in her sister's life that something was wrong. And that troubled her deeply, yet she couldn't bring herself to share these things with Ashley in full. For now, she could only bring them to Yeshua.

I guess it's time to join the others on the field, Tina thought. *Everyone's about to arrive.*

As Tina approached the players, she noticed the newcomer's captivating charm. Her heart skipped a beat, but Yeshua whispered to her: "Keep your eyes on me." He also reminded her of his promise to never leave or forsake her. She took comfort in this reassurance as she continued walking towards the group.

In the distance, Tina spotted her sister's car parked in the lot. Ashley was getting out with a group of their friends.

Just then, the newcomer's gaze shifted towards Ashley, and suddenly Tina noticed her sister's fluid and graceful walk. Her blonde hair glistened in the sunlight, gathered in a loose side ponytail.

Trent also noticed Aaron gazing towards Ashley and shouted, "Proximity alert!"

Without warning, Trent, Josh, and Ethan tackled Aaron to the ground with such great force that it knocked the wind out of him.

Tina sensed that the men had tackled the newcomer as a warning. They treated women starkly differently than most other men and challenged behaviours that indicated lustful thoughts.

As Tina quietly arrived beside the pile of men on the grass, she couldn't help but feel a sense of relief that Aaron's focus had shifted back to the game.

"Our sisters are priceless treasures," Trent said to Aaron with a stern, serious tone.

Josh nodded in agreement. "One that we as brothers are responsible to guard and protect."

"So you'd better watch yourself," Ethan added, his voice laced with warning. "Will you turn from going your way and back to the God who made you? For the kingdom and family of heaven is at hand."

Arden, a young and energetic member of the group, ran forward and jumped atop the pile before Aaron could catch his breath enough to respond.

The air around them was still as they all waited for Aaron to speak.

"So what you're saying is that we were made to protect and defend, not to take advantage. How come no one has ever told me that?" Aaron finally managed, his breaths coming in gasps.

A memory of Claudia in the hospital room, fighting for her life, flashed in his mind. Guilt pricked his conscious once more.

As Tina listened to the words spoken, they reverberated through her, striking a chord deep in her heart. She knew the words were true, that they were a reflection of the original design of men. Every man was born with a purpose to protect and defend, to seek justice, to love mercy, and to walk humbly with God.

However, it was disheartening to see so many men living in a manner that was the complete antithesis to this design. Tina couldn't help but feel this newcomer was one of them. Something about his demeanour made her feel wary, almost as if he was similar to those who had already caused her sister so much devastation.

Trent, Ethan, Josh, and Arden were different. They went out of their way to protect and defend the women around them. It was if they were sisters. They cherished, respected, treasured, protected, and honoured each one of them.

FIVE

The air was filled with a palpable excitement as the group gathered to play soccer on this sunny day. After exchanging introductions, they decided to split into two teams. Ethan and Josh were chosen as team captains. After a quick huddle, Josh's team adorned bright blue jersey pinnies that stood out against the lush green field.

The players were equally matched and worked together flawlessly, moving back and forth across the field in a coordinated effort. Ethan passed the ball to Trent, who had Arden in front of him and tried to shield him with his back while passing the ball to Ashley. Ashley received the ball and attempted a quick shot on goal. Although it missed, luckily Sarah was nearby to take advantage of the opportunity and kicked the ball into the corner of the net, earning her team a point.

Tina gained control of the ball and passed to Ethan, who took it and ran for a while before passing to an available teammate. As they coursed up the field, Ethan helped protect the ball. After a faked shot to Tina, he took a clean shot on net and scored, causing an eruption of cheers, high fives, and compliments from both his teammates and members of the opposing team.

The sun shone brilliantly, casting dazzling circles of light and rainbow colours over the ground. The players' laughter reverberated through the air, and even the wind seemed to join in the fun, playfully blowing Josh's white hat off his head for the third time.

The simple act of playing soccer together brought broad grins to everyone's faces and joy to the heart, lifting their spirits. For Tina, it was a true blessing to be able to play soccer with her brothers and sisters in Christ. Her heart overflowed with joy and thanksgiving to God for this adopted family.

She keenly observed that the bond between the friends grew stronger whenever they gathered to play soccer, wrestle, tease, or participate in sports drills. These activities tested their strength and built trust, reminding them that they could always rely on each other through thick and thin because they followed Yeshua Christ as the Lord of their lives. They regarded one another as belonging to he who had bought each with the precious treasure of his blood.

As a team and family, each member had an important role to play in fostering healthy character growth. Living shoulder to shoulder, circumstances sometimes tested them, but these were a crucial aspect of purifying their hearts. By challenging each other's behaviours and attitudes, they looked out for one another and built a strong foundation of trust and support to last a lifetime.

The warm summer day eventually came to an end, but Josh, Aaron, Arden, Trent, and Ethan lingered on the ground. They didn't seem to mind the grass stains and dirt on their clothes as they lay basking in each other's company. They sipped water and bantered amongst themselves—except for Arden and Aaron, who quietly observed the others.

"Josh, would you have held onto the ball so well if someone had threatened your coffee?" Trent asked jokingly.

"Nah. I would have been even more focused and quick. Protecting my coffee is a top priority!" Josh tossed the ball to Ethan. "Gotta keep your one-touch wonder going!"

The group burst out laughing.

"We should hide the coffee next time," Trent suggested.

Josh shook his finger. "Then no more coffee runs for you!"

"I'd swipe your card and order coffee for the whole city, Josh," said Trent. "You have the power of blessing!"

That's when Ethan noticed that Arden seemed to be lost in thought. "Earth to Arden! Are you on cloud nine thinking about your girlfriend?"

Arden snapped out of his reverie. "Not this time, Ethan. Sometimes we can get so caught up in the details that we forget to appreciate the bigger picture. The wonder of life is full of potential… full of dreams. It's amazing that we can have fellowship and build family bonds with one another."

"Isn't it a little early for us to dive so deep into a philosophical discussion?" Aaron asked.

"No," Arden replied. "Most of us are already swimming in the deep waters of life. We need to learn how to navigate the stronger currents. If we don't, we'll hit a rock sooner or later. Even the strongest of men and women can be overwhelmed by the storms that come."

Aaron fell silent as he sat cross-legged on the lush green grass, his eyes fixed on this unusual group of men. They were his friends now, but he couldn't help feeling like an outsider. They laughed and joked, and he once again felt the sense of unease that had been gnawing at him for weeks. He felt like he was living someone else's life, wearing a costume that didn't quite fit.

As the sun set, casting a warm golden glow over the soccer field, the trees rustled in the breeze, whispering a soft melody. Birds flitted from branch to branch, their songs mingling.

Aaron felt a pang of envy as he watched his new friends. They seemed so at ease, so content, while he felt like he was constantly searching for something he couldn't name.

Trent's face lit up as a butterfly landed on a nearby flower. The insect's wings unfolded to reveal a riot of colours and patterns.

"Look at that," he said, his voice filled with wonder. "Isn't it amazing? How can anyone look at this and not believe in a higher power?"

Josh grinned and tossed the ball at Trent. "Hey, bug man, don't get too lost in your thoughts. We need you to score some goals."

Aaron felt a smile tug at the corners of his mouth. Despite his doubt and fear, he felt a sense of warmth and belonging in these men's company. He wasn't ready to leave, not yet. He wanted to stay and soak up every moment of this camaraderie and mutual respect. He wanted to learn from these men, to understand what it meant to truly live.

As the sun finally sank below the horizon, he closed his eyes and breathed in the scent of grass and trees, feeling more alive than he had in a long time.

"When I was leaving my former lifestyle of drugs and hard alcohol, I remember that the cravings were so intense and impossible to fight on my own strength," Josh said. "Yet Yeshua was there, encouraging me each day to make better choices and ease off those things incrementally. When the day came that I was off drugs and alcohol entirely, Father Light challenged me to be an encouraging support for troubled teens and youth, to be the kind of person Yeshua was for me in their lives. It actively makes a difference."

The mention of Father Light seemed to have a particular effect on Aaron, who became tense and focused. It was a reminder of his quest to serve his master above all else.

Ethan noticed Aaron's change in demeanour.

"Hey buddy," he said soothingly. "We're all part of Father Light's family. Be still and know that his light is good. He has drawn us to himself and adopted us into his family. For it was his great delight to do so."

As Ethan spoke, his words calmed Aaron, who began to relax. Aaron had been feeling aimless for weeks, wandering in a metaphorical desert, unable to find his way out. And now he had stumbled across a group of men who got along so well that he felt like he was finally drinking pure water again. These men had such an unusual energy that Aaron couldn't help but be intrigued. He wanted to know more about them and their family. What made them so different from everyone else he had ever met?

Suddenly, the men broke into song. Aaron's train of thought derailed as he stopped to listen, completely mesmerized. Trent's voice was particularly enchanting.

Aaron's heart swelled with emotion. The more they sang, the more everything around them seemed to join in with the joyful melody. He decided to let his questions wait and just enjoy their time together. He closed his eyes and relished in this sense of belonging.

As the group finished, Aaron sat up straight them with a mixture of curiosity, longing, and turbulence in his heart.

"Who were you all singing about?" he asked, hoping to learn more about this mysterious song.

During the ensuing conversation, the men spoke of their adoptive Father Light, who had brought them into his family. Upon closer listening, however, he realized they were discussing the rival family.

Aaron couldn't help but see an opportunity to gather intel, and potentially even earn a reward from his master.

"Can you tell me more about this Father Light?" Aaron asked when the conversation hit a lull.

They began to tell the story of the one who had created them, who had seen that they were lost and in need of rescue. They had once been held captive by a rival family, their lives in danger. Father Light had loved them so much that he'd paid to buy them back and make them his own. They believed that Father Light had seen a priceless treasure deep within them, something worth redeeming.

Father Light had traded the life of the only perfect man in exchange for all of humanity. This man was Father Light's eldest Son, Yeshua, who had willingly given his life so they could be set free from the grip of sin and death. He had taken their place on the cross and paid the price for their sins. Yeshua had suffered and died so they could live a good and adventurous life.

In the eyes of these men, Father Light had made a way for them to achieve the life they had always dreamed of but hadn't been able to achieve on their own.

The story of Yeshua didn't end with his death, though, for he was raised to life in power by Father Light to confirm the men's adoption. Yeshua had defeated death and fulfilled his prophecy by rising again, his resurrection serving as undeniable proof of his divine nature and the sufficiency of his sacrifice to save mankind.

"To receive the gift of salvation Yeshua has purchased for us with his blood, all we must do is accept the invitation of a new life, turning away from our sinful ways towards God, who created all things," explained Trent. "By doing so, we become children of Father Light and heirs to his kingdom. We owe him our lives and can bask in the freedom and joy he offers."

Ethan nodded vigorously. "Father Light has created everything and has a vision to complete all things. He extends an invitation to all, asking them to turn away from their own ways and return to his original intent for their lives. Through his redemptive plan, he restores what was once broken beyond repair. In fact, he even gives us new names, transforming our character and motivating to become more like him as we trust."

Aaron stood up, his face as blank as a mask. He needed some time and space to think through what he had just heard.

"Well, guys, it's been great meeting you all," Aaron said, trying to hide his inner turmoil. "Thanks for the talk and a great game."

Ethan smiled. "We'll be back here tomorrow morning at 10:30 if you're interested in a rematch."

"Maybe. I might take you up on that offer." Aaron got ready to walk away, but first he shook everyone's hand.

As Aaron left the field, Arden watched him closely, feeling troubled by the darkness he saw in their new friend's life. He knew what it was like to live with such deep-seated darkness, having experienced it during his own days with the rival family. Arden was all too familiar with the consequences of his choices.

He felt the need to keep an eye on Aaron.

Later that day, Arden returned home and went into his bedroom. He stopped in the middle of the room and tapped a floorboard. Underneath it was a secret box in which he kept items he had secretly developed after his work for the rival family. He knew from experience that he might one day have need of them.

He pulled up the board and removed the box, opening the lid to reveal its contents. Inside he found a taser with an ankle strap and modified needle. The needle held his own unique formula, one strong enough to drop even Superman.

Thinking hard, he decided to temporarily store both items in his soccer bag, just in case Aaron returned and caused trouble the next day. He was determined to be prepared for whatever trouble may come.

The next morning dawned bright and clear. As planned, the friends planned to meet for soccer at 10:30, in the same field as the day before. Shortly after ten o'clock, Arden arrived with his duffel bag. He found Trent lying on the grass, reading a book and enjoying the sunshine.

Arden put his bag down by the net, changed into his soccer cleats, and began his warmup stretches. Once done, he opened the bag and briefly looked over to see what Trent was doing. He had lain the book aside and had shut his eyes, enjoying the moment.

Arden rolled up his sweatpants, then removed the modified taser, ankle strap, and modified needle from the bag and velcroed it to his right foot. He rolled the material back down to seamlessly cover the nimble design of his invention. After that, he pulled out his soccer ball and rolled it along the grass in front of the soccer net.

"Come on, Trent, let's get in some more warmup and practice shots before the others get here and we have to share with Fancy Feet!"

It was a running joke in the group. Ethan's fancy soccer moves had led to him being given that nickname.

"Great idea, Arden. You're on!" Trent got to his feet and stretched his tall frame. "Speaking of fancy feet, I have yet to master ball control with Ethan's level of skill."

Soon after, the men lined up to take shots on net. Trent was selected as the first goalie, and Arden was the first to shoot. They decided to alternate every five to ten minutes.

Midway through Arden's time, he moved the ball backward to practice his long shot. The net they were using wasn't far from the forest's edge, where the grass was long and the tall trees provided shade. He misjudged the distance, though, and the ball flew in an arc over the net. It landed in the tree, rolled down a long branch, and fell to the ground.

When it finally landed, the men heard a surprising shout that turned into a growl.

Without warning, a dark figure ran towards them from the underbrush. The man rushed at Arden and punched him in the nose. The pain made Arden stumble back for a moment and briefly struggle to find his hidden weapon.

That moment was all it took for the intruder to jump on Trent and knock him to the ground, punching and kicking him repeatedly.

Arden finally found his weapon and jumped on the figure's back. He jabbed the needle hard into the man's hip. The drug quickly took effect and knocked out their assailant.

That's when he realized it was Aaron.

Seeing that Aaron had knocked Trent out, Arden safely rolled Aaron off their friend. Afterward he sighed, wishing he hadn't been right, and pulled out his phone. He called the emergency operator to request police assistance and an ambulance to take the pair to the hospital.

During the wait for help to arrive, Arden kept a close eye on his friend Trent. He also sent a quick emergency text to the others and wiped some rebellious tears from his eyes.

SIX

A aron forced his eyelids open to the near-blinding midafternoon sun. He quickly shut them again and looked for relief from the throbbing pain in his head, which felt like a four-drum band following a trumpeter. He felt a hard surface underneath him and a rough blanket near his feet. Opening his eyes a crack again, he registered that he was in a jail cell.

What had happened? Aaron couldn't remember, but the pain increased. The hard cot and barred window told him he'd done something terrible.

You killed somebody, the voice in his head said. *You don't deserve to live!*

The thought brought shame and condemnation.

A memory flashed: his bloody and bruised knuckles hitting Trent in the face. Again, again, and again. The urge to kill swelled within. He had absolutely no control over his own body.

Another flash: Trent helping a lady to her feet from a wheelchair in a café as she shouted, "I'm healed! I'm healed!"

Sorrow, guilt, and remorse filled his heart. He'd killed goofy, gold-natured Trent.

Aaron sat up on the hard cot and gathered the sheets together. Grabbing the first and tearing the cotton into long strips, he thought of one possibility. It offered a tempting sort of relief.

A bunch of torn strips later, he heard a squeak down the hall, then the scrape of metal as the dividing door opened. Aaron heard footsteps on the cement floor, followed by the distinctive sound of bubble gum being chewed, blown, and popped.

Josh appeared in front of the door with a guard.

"Hey Aaron," the man said, briefly glancing at the strips of sheets in Aaron's lap. "Can I tell you about what Yeshua has done for me?"

Aaron paused what he was doing and shrugged. "Sure, man, you can."

"Yeshua gave me a second chance and encouraged me to change my ways. I'd been addicted to pain pills and alcohol, living in depression. Then Yeshua called me by name and my parents got their son back and set my feet on a different path. I know he wants to do the same thing for you." Josh paused to let that sink in. "Here comes Ethan."

Down the hall, a key slid into the lock and the door opened once again. The squeak of sneakers on the tile indicated the arrival of another visitor.

Soon Ethan stood before Aaron's jail cell, positioned beside the stone-faced guard.

"Hey, Aaron, your bail has been posted," Ethan said. "You've been released into my care."

That was the last thing Aaron had expected to hear. He felt bewildered and shocked. "What? How can that be?"

Patiently, Ethan explained. "Your bail has been posted and I'm bringing you home to my place."

"But why, after what I've done?"

"Because God's love brings redemption to his enemies."

Ethan carefully watched Aaron's face. His heart was so full of compassion towards the inmate, even though he'd tried to kill Trent that very morning.

After leaving the jail, Josh and Ethan took Aaron to pick up some lunch. They bought some sandwiches at a drive-through, the mouth-watering aroma of food filling the vehicle. Ethan said a quiet blessing as they pulled into the parking lot and stopped. He and Josh began to eat right away, but Aaron didn't so much as touch his food.

"I want to go see Trent," Aaron said at last.

This didn't surprise Ethan, but he did have to respect the agreement he'd made with the police regarding Aaron's conditional release.

"Unfortunately, you're under investigation for Trent's attempted murder," Ethan explained. "You aren't allowed to be in the same vicinity as him."

"You mean I didn't succeed in killing Trent?"

"No, but he's in critical condition. You aren't allowed to see him. We can meet with the other guys outside the hospital for an update, though."

When they got to the hospital, they sat on a bench next to a tree near the hospital entrance. That's where they were sitting when Arden came outside and saw them. Without thinking, he ran over to Aaron and punched him in the face. Arden then pulled back his arm for another forceful hook, but this time it connected with Ethan's chin; Ethan had stepped between the pair. Now Ethan and Aaron had matching bruises.

Arden's shock at hitting his friend brought him to his senses. He stepped back.

Josh grasped his arm. "Come on, man. This is not who you are."

"I deserved those punches," Aaron whispered. "You didn't have to step in and take the punch, Ethan."

"Mercy means getting what we don't deserve," said Ethan. "Father Light has lavished both mercy and grace upon me. Extending the same to others is part of my new life of service to my master. Who is your master, Aaron?"

Before he could answer, Tina ran up. She was still dressed in her uniform from her shift at the café where she worked.

She first turned to Aaron and Ethan. "Put some ice on those bruises."

Everyone stood in place for a moment, surprised at her taking charge.

"The Holy Trio has Trent's life in their hands," she continued. "I'll stay with Trent through the night and call if any changes occur. Arden, come by the hospital first thing tomorrow and swap me out. Ethan and Josh will take the subsequent shifts. Now, Aaron…" Tina paused to look him in the eyes. "Stay at Ethan's for the time being. Please listen to him share God's love, mercy, and grace with you. You might receive and believe these for yourself. God is knocking on your door."

With that, the group split into three. Tina went into the hospital while the two pairs of men walked towards their respective cars.

From the hospital, Josh drove Arden into the country. Before heading to Ethan's place, they decided to stop at a hiking trail.

"Come on, bro, let get this off your chest," Josh said.

They left the car and sat on the grass to stare up at the stars.

"Where is the justice in this?" Arden demanded, his anger simmering. "Don't you care that this loser tried to kill Trent this morning?"

Father, how do I respond? Josh prayed. Soon, in the stillness, the answer came.

"Arden, the God who made us is passionate about justice and mercy," he said after a moment. "A person can only live in wickedness for so long before God has enough and brings them to justice, in part with the hope that they'll turn from their evil ways back to him. Remember that none of us deserve his mercy. But it was given to us anyway, out of his pure love. The Holy Spirit takes us by the hand and firmly leads us into a changed life. At some point along the way, we are all given an experience that causes us to trust God. Yeshua, God's Son, died in our place. Our lives as believers in him are intended to display a different reality than the dark chaos around us. For Aaron's sake, we must follow Christ as our lord and master, even when our circumstances and emotions try to convince us otherwise. We are called to live for the Holy Trio's honour, not for ourselves, but for Yeshua, who while he was on the earth made his life's purpose and focus the will of Father Light." He took a deep breath. "Arden, we have been forgiven much through God's mercy. Remember that and forgive Aaron out of mercy also. Judging others and living in darkness is not how we've been called to live."

Arden stared up at the stars twinkling in the night. The moon was a bright sign of God's faithfulness, yet he felt that the Holy Trio was far away, even though in reality they were closer than Arden's next breath.

"I'm sorry, Lord, for following my foolish ways and taking matters into my own hands, for holding bitterness and unforgiveness in my heart," Arden prayed aloud. "Even though I was guilty of living the same way, you forgave me, Lord. I choose to forgive Aaron for trying to kill Trent."

Arden heard the answer as it resonated in his heart and mind: *"I love and forgive you, my son. Allow my love in your life to be forged stronger in the fire you are walking through."*

Arden was reminded of what Yeshua did on the cross. He even imagined being there. At that moment, he let go of the offence in his heart.

At Ethan's house, Aaron struggled to understand why the man had helped him. The reasons sounded crazy, like nothing he'd ever heard of before. His new friend's unique behaviour had created within Aaron a hunger to hear more. He hadn't deserved Ethan's help.

The two men sat across from each other in the living room, with Aaron seated in a chair facing away from the window while Ethan lounged on the couch across from him. The men each held a Bible. A half-filled cup of lukewarm tea sat on the table next to Aaron.

"Please, go over this again," Aaron said quietly. "I still don't understand why you bailed me out of jail and took that punch. How is this man's life, Yeshua, relevant to what you've done for me?"

Aaron held a package of frozen peas to his lip and the side of his face. Ethan had a similar bag of mixed veggies over his eye.

"Entering into my family starts with turning back from one's wicked ways to face Father Light, the Creator God who made all things, as we discussed yesterday after soccer," said Ethan. "My Lord Yeshua has extended mercy to me and led me into a new way of living. This includes giving the same to others who don't deserve it and not living for myself. By his death on the cross and resurrection, he defeated death. So doing what is wrong in God's sight is no longer part of my life. It has been removed, and I stand before God no longer condemned but forgiven. I helped you to demonstrate, Aaron, that mercy and grace are freely available to you by faith in Yeshua as Lord. You don't have to earn it, but you get to receive it as a priceless gift. This new life we get to live is so very different from the culture around us."

Ethan stood up, stretched, and grabbed their half-filled mugs of tea.

"I'm going to add some hot water," he said. "Feel free to use the washroom. It's down the hall, the first door on your left."

Aaron also got up and stretched his entire frame. "That sounds like a good idea. I'll be right back."

Suddenly, without warning, the window cracked. Aaron fell to the ground and blood began to pool beneath him.

It was a bullet, passing through Aaron's body and hitting Ethan. Ethan fell to the ground, dropping their mugs. The pottery shattered into tiny pieces.

Father, make something beautiful out of these broken pieces, Ethan prayed as he lay dying. *Yeshua, I will see you sooner than I thought, sooner than I planned. It's been an honour to lose my life for your sake, Lord, and join in your suffering. Please look after my brothers and sisters when I'm gone. Comfort them in their grief.*

Aaron looked over at him. "Ethan?"

"Still here, man. Lord Yeshua, our lives are in your hands," he said in a soft voice. "After all, the blood of Christ and the martyrs was the foundation of the early Christian church. Lord, it's a privilege to be counted among them. Yet there are things I still want to do with you on this earth."

Aaron's chest felt tight. "Yeshua, help us."

"Aaron, the cross of Yeshua is the only part of any belief system where love, mercy, and grace all meet. In times like these, our love for God and others is forged in the fires of affliction." Ethan took a shaky breath. "Father Light, forgive those who have done this. They know not what they do."

"I'm sorry to have gotten you shot, Ethan. It's my fault that this happened."

"This is not entirely your fault. You made your choices, and they made theirs. There must be free will for love to be possible. Where free will exists, there is the opportunity for evil, violence, and hate."

Josh was driving Arden home when he suddenly sensed an urgent prompting from the Holy Spirit to go to Ethan's place.

"Arden, I need to go to Ethan's right now," he said. "Something's happening!"

Just as quickly, Arden's heart was blanketed with peace. "I'll come with you. Tina asked me to go swap with her at dawn anyway."

With that, Josh turned the car around and began to head in the opposite direction.

"Are you still with me, Aaron?"

Aaron coughed with a dry mouth. "Yes, I am. Ethan, what does it mean to live?"

"To live is to know God, who made all creation and gave us life. If you ever pause and consider all of creation, you will be able to see our Creator God's divine power and glory. The full scope of life *is* God, the one who made us honour the Holy Trio with everything within us."

"If this God is as good as you say, I want to know him."

"He's even better. What you've heard is only the tip of the iceberg." Ethan coughed. "Father Light is perfect and has had a plan since before the foundation of the world. That plan involves adopting us as his children. Yeshua, the Son of God, was the creative inspiration for all things. He came to the earth to reveal the Father's Light. The Holy Spirit has characteristics like a man and a woman, which is why there is a third pronoun in the original Hebrew to describe the Holy Spirit in the Bible. He is tender and powerful. All three members of the Trio live in constant closeness and community."

"It sounds out of this world, man," Aaron slurred.

Lord Yeshua, please remember me after I die, he prayed.

"Ethan, if I don't make it, please tell Trent I'm sorry."

"You'll make it, Aaron, for you are discovering what it means to live truly. To live is Christ; to die is gain by being reunited with the Holy Trio."

The doorbell rang.

Josh and Arden stood at the door to Ethan's duplex, wondering why no one was answering the bell. When Josh looked over and noticed the hole in the living room window, he realized what had happened. He quickly opened the door with his spare key.

Inside the living room, they found both Ethan and Aaron on the floor, bleeding. Josh's medical training kicked in.

"Arden, grab towels from the bathroom and put pressure on Aaron's wound." Josh pulled out his phone and called 911.

"Operator."

"Hi, I need an ambulance to 721 Radiant Road. Two men have been shot, and one's breathing is shallow. We are putting pressure on the wound to try and slow the bleeding. Please hurry."

Josh hung up the phone as Arden returned with the towels and handed him a few. Then Arden bent down next to Aaron and pressed a towel over the wound in the man's shoulder.

"Hey man, the calvary's coming."

Aaron groaned. "Arden, I'm so sorry for trying to kill Trent."

"I forgive you, Aaron," Arden breathed. "And Yeshua does, too."

"We've been talking about him." Aaron smiled. "In fact, Ethan has been sharing so much with me and about what it means to truly live."

"I'm sorry for hitting you earlier, Aaron. Even though I was angry, it was wrong. I have no right to get offended like that."

"I forgive you also, brother." Aaron coughed, and in the distance he heard an abundance of police sirens. "Yeshua is our only perfect Saviour."

SEVEN

As the first rays of sunlight peeked through the window and illuminated the hospital room, Tina stirred from her slumber, grabbed her bag, and trudged out into the hallway. She walked down the corridor, her footsteps echoing on the tiles.

She was heading towards the cafeteria, hoping to grab a quick breakfast, when she caught sight of something that gave her pause. Arden was seated in a chair in the waiting area, his shirt stained with blood. He stared down at his hands, seemingly lost in thought. He looked dazed, as if he was in shock.

Tina's heart raced as she approached him. "Arden, what happened?"

Arden looked up at her with tears in his brown eyes. "Ethan and Aaron were shot. Josh and I found them. They're both in emergency surgery now."

"Whose blood is on your shirt?"

"Aaron's."

Tina sat on the sofa beside Arden. Without a word, she opened her arms to give him a hug. He accepted and cried in her arms.

"I forgave him for hurting Trent," he sobbed. "He and Ethan were talking about Yeshua while waiting for help. What a way to celebrate coming home into the kingdom…"

Arden's voice dripped with sarcasm. Tina knew how close he was to both Trent and Ethan. The bond of brotherhood between them was deep.

Tears slipped unheeded from their eyes. There were no words to express the emotions both felt. In that instant, the Holy Spirit brought them comfort through each other's faith and their shared experience. Together they cried, quietly prayed, and waited.

"I am with you," Yeshua whispered.

In his hospital bed, deep in a dream, Trent sensed Lord Yeshua approach him from behind. He placed a hand on the top of Trent's head, and Trent felt electric power from God flow through his entire being.

"Arise and shine with my glory," he heard the Lord speak. *"Your time has not yet come to return home to me."*

Although Trent could hear the Father's voice, he couldn't see him.

"I love you dearly, my son. I'm proud that you have humbly chosen to walk through life with me."

Trent's eyes shot open and he recognized where he was, hooked up to IVs and monitoring equipment. His mouth burst into a goofy grin full of thankful praise to God. He immediately began thanking the Lord for everything he'd done—for every blessing, seen and unseen, for all the wonder, mystery, and glory all around.

"Thank you, God, for children and for coffee!" he finished, his voice getting so loud that it soon awoke Tina and Arden, who had fallen asleep in the chairs out in the hallway.

An Indigenous man was sleeping a few seats down from them in the hallway, and Trent's shout inadvertently woke him up, along with Arden and Tina. The man wore a baseball hat with the words *Native Pride* written on it.

"Christianity has caused my people enough trouble," the man mumbled. "We don't need to hear any more of that bull."

Feeling the urgency to make things right, Tina knelt on the floor before the man and looked him directly in the eye. She spoke with sincerity and genuine grief.

"Sir, I'm deeply sorry for how you and your people have been introduced to God and Yeshua. I don't believe they ever intend to force themselves on anyone. It would have been so much better for my people to reveal God to your people through stories, shared lives, and honouring friendship rather than selfishly taking what they wanted from you and tearing apart your families."

The man's dark eyes lightened and began to moisten with tears.

"Thank you," he said.

With that, the man stood up and walked down the hall towards the cafeteria.

Arden stood to go after him, but Tina grabbed his hand.

"Don't," she said. "Let's give the man and the Holy Spirit space. We don't know what lies in this man's heart. Only the Great Spirit does. Anyone can know God's nature by taking a long and thoughtful look at creation, God's wondrous handiwork. Yet ultimately we have been given free will in how we live, think about God, and relate to each other."

Arden stretched out his hand, offering it to Tina. She grasped it tightly and pulled herself up from the floor.

Together, they walked into Trent's room, where a nurse, whose badge read "Rosie," was standing by the bed, checking Trent's vitals.

Despite the recent life-threatening episode he had experienced, Trent seemed calm and composed, almost serene. As he looked at Rosie's face, he spoke softly, his voice a curious blend of seriousness and humour.

"Rosie, your beauty is angelic. You're a true masterpiece, an extraordinary treasure unlike any other. As a woman, you're worth more than all the treasures in the world."

Rosie's eyes filled with tears, but she didn't say a word. When she finished her task, she left the room silently.

Rosie soon found herself standing in front of a sink in the women's bathroom. She turned the knob and cold water gushed out, splashing onto her face. As she looked up at the mirror, she saw her reflection staring back at her—and her heart sank. Her eyes were red and puffy, the evidence of the tears she had shed after hearing Trent's words. Her once-smooth complexion was dotted with pimples and blackheads, visible signs of her nervous fear and constant anxiety. Her freckles and curly red hair, which she had always disliked, seemed to taunt; they had never won her any favours on the playground. Dark bags hung heavily under her eyes while worry lines creased her forehead, making her look older than she was. To add to her woes, she couldn't help but notice some premature grey hairs starting to sprout.

Rosie dropped down to the bathroom floor and huddled in front of the wall, overcome by feelings of worthlessness and despair. The walls seemed to close in on her as she struggled to comprehend why she felt so unlovable. All she knew was that she felt used and discarded, like a worthless object. Her thoughts raced, causing her anxiety, which in turn made her stomach churn.

Suddenly feeling a wave of nausea overtake her, she rushed to the nearest stall.

Rosie had been going through a tough time, feeling like she had little control over her life. However, she had found a way to regulate her eating habits to give herself a sense of control.

Unfortunately, this was the third time she had thrown up this week, and it was only Tuesday.

As she retched over the toilet bowl, she heard the bathroom door open. She didn't care who it was. She was too consumed by her own pain to pay attention.

"Rosie, do you need a hug?" a kind voice asked.

It was Tina, Trent's friend.

Rosie's tears welled up in her eyes as she nodded. "Yes."

Without another word, Tina walked over and wrapped her arms around her. Rosie felt like a small child as Tina held her tightly, stroking her hair and rubbing her back. She cried and cried as a deep well of pain opened inside her. There was no stopping it.

She didn't care that her tears and snot were getting all over the side of Tina's shirt. All she knew was that she needed someone to hold her and tell her that she was loved.

Arden's heart skipped a beat when he saw Trent alive and well. The relief he felt was immense, and he couldn't help but let out a sigh.

However, the moment of solace was short-lived as the activity in the ICU suddenly picked up. Nurses and doctors frantically rushed into one of the other rooms, and Arden couldn't help but feel a knot form in his stomach. He needed to find out where Aaron and Ethan were staying. He couldn't shake his feeling of unease.

As he stood frozen in the doorway of Trent's room, he heard a call from the intercom: "Code blue! ICU 4!" The same message repeated moments only later, and Rosie stepped out of the washroom with tears in her eyes. She wiped them away and left to attend to her duties.

Arden slowly began walking down the hall, but everything seemed to move in slow motion. The atmosphere was heavy and Arden felt a wave of sadness wash over him.

Rosie rushed to the ICU, Room 4, where the trauma team had already taken a step back from the patient's bed.

"Time of death, 09:32," the doctor declared sombrely.

Rosie looked up and noticed a mysterious figure lingering in the room. She squinted, unable to get a good look at it, but it seemed to be dressed in a dark cloak.

Looking back down, she noted the time being written in the patient's file by the doctor. Sadly, the staff filed out.

When Rosie left the room, she found Tina waiting outside. Tina had stopped in her tracks, hesitating in front of the door.

"Ethan," she gasped, trying to look past Rosie to the body lying in the bed.

Surprised, Rosie turned to face her, wondering who this Ethan fellow was.

"Excuse me," said Tina. "Who's staying in this room?"

Rosie went back into the room and gazed down at the patient's file, still resting on a clipboard at the foot of the room. Confused and startled, she saw the patient's name: Ethan.

"Can I please have a moment alone with him?" Tina asked. "He's a friend of mine."

"Yes," Rosie said, backing off so Tina could get past her. "But someone will be around shortly to take the body to the morgue."

Rosie felt a strong urge to stay with Tina in the room where Ethan lay motionless on the bed. She came to a stop at the foot of the bed while Tina took the man's hand.

"Ethan, I don't think it's your time to go home yet," Tina said with tears in her eyes. "There's still so much left unfinished here."

Rosie could sense the deep connection between these two. What was it?

Tina closed her eyes and began to pray. "Father Light, I thank you for the gifts of your Son and precious Spirit in our lives. I am grateful that the three of you made this man, gave him life, and have led him into mine." She paused before continuing, her voice carrying a slight quiver. "The life of this man belongs to you, Father, as one ransomed with a price and devoted to you. I ask as your daughter, will you make this dead man walk again and breathe new life into these dry bones? For your honour and glory, God, not my will but yours be done." Softly, her voice hardly audible, she added in a whisper: "Not my will but yours be done, Father. I entrust my heart into your care."

Rosie observed the gravity of the moment as Tina spoke with authority and conviction, her voice growing louder and more confident.

"Ethan, rise up and live in Yeshua's name!" she suddenly commanded boldly. "Your time has not yet come! Live once more for the Lord's honour and glory."

The room fell silent as Tina clasped Ethan's hand, her eyes closed in deep concentration.

Meanwhile, in response to Tina's prayers, the Holy Spirit breathed new life into Ethan's lifeless body.

Rosie watched in amazement as Ethan's chest began to rise and fall with newfound breath. His colour returned and his eyes opened slowly, taking in the unfamiliar surroundings.

Tina's face lit up with relief and gratitude as tears streamed down her cheeks.

"Thank you, Lord, for this miracle," she whispered.

Rosie stood awestruck at what she had just witnessed, feeling a newfound sense of faith and hope. It was a moment that would stay with her the rest of her life, a testament to the power of prayer and the unwavering faith of those who believe.

Tina's gaze shifted to the spot where she had noticed the cloaked figure lurking, but it had vanished without a trace.

Meanwhile, Ethan was gasping for air, struggling to breathe. Rosie rushed to his side and placed her hand on his neck to check for a pulse.

"I've got a pulse! I've got a pulse!" she cried out, her voice catching the attention of the ICU doctor down the hall.

The time on the clock read 9:37 a.m.

Even twelve hours later, the events of the day lingered in Rosie's mind. She couldn't shake off the memory of witnessing a man who was supposed to have been dead come back to life. The desire to understand what had happened and why stirred within her like a burning flame.

As Rosie walked to Ethan's room, she couldn't help but recall the image of her own father passing away in a hospital bed. How could the man she had seen today come back to life when her own father hadn't been so fortunate? How was it even possible? Her questions were endless, but answers were nowhere to be found.

Rosie couldn't help but feel envious and angry at the care Tina had shown for her friend. She'd had an equally special bond with her father. Why hadn't that been enough to save him?

With a loud bang, she shut her locker door and headed back up to the fourth floor, determined to find the answers she sought.

Soon she was standing outside the door to Ethan's room, her hand hovering over the doorknob. Music emanated from within, a soulful melody accompanied by a deep, resonant voice. As she listened, she realized it was Ethan singing. She was struck by the power, peace, and deep emotion in his voice.

Pushing the door open a crack, Rosie peered inside. Ethan lay on the bed, his arms raised over his head, eyes closed in concentration. One arm was slightly lower than the other, connected to the IVs that were keeping him alive.

As the man sang, Rosie noticed the passion and conviction in his face, even though his eyes were shut. She felt a pang of longing; Ethan was alive in a way she had never seen before.

She hesitated, not sure whether she should interrupt, but ultimately she decided to knock on the door regardless. She knocked twice and saw Ethan stop the music and lower his arms.

"Come in," he called out.

As Rosie entered the room, she introduced herself. She sat on the edge of the bed, hesitating before asking her first question.

"How is it that you're still alive?" she wondered aloud. "Your heart stopped beating."

Ethan's face lit up with a smile, his eyes sparkling with joy. "I owe my life to God's Spirit. My friend Tina had faith in Yeshua, and through her faith God brought me back to life. It wasn't my own strength that saved me. It was a miracle by the Holy Spirit of might, not by anyone's effort. I'm grateful for every breath I take."

Rosie took this in, trying to make sense of it.

"Have you ever experienced the awe-inspiring beauty of a starry night?" Ethan asked. "Or a breathtaking sunset?"

Rosie thought back to her memories of running on the beach with her father, watching the sun disappear into the ocean. She nodded.

"Well, Rosie, that same sense of wonder and amazement you feel when you gaze upon the beauty of nature is God's power at work. We may not be able to see it, but we can feel and experience it. It's like the words we speak and hear with our ears; they can have a profound impact on our lives, even if we can't see them."

As Rosie gazed into Ethan's eyes, she saw a curious mix of passion, fire, and compassion. Something about him stirred her curiosity. How was it that he had come back to life? She still didn't fully understand.

"Rosie, I can tell you about the one who brought me back to life," he said with a hint of mystery in his voice. "The choice will be yours whether to trust him or not."

Rosie knew all too well that trust was a risky business. She had been burned before, and the scars still lingered. But there was something about this man, something that drew her in and refused to let go. She crossed the room and sat down in the empty visitor's chair, her eyes fixed on Ethan's.

"Please tell me more about this God of yours," she said, her voice barely above a whisper.

Ethan spoke with conviction, passion flaring from his brown eyes as he shared the gospel. "According to the creation story, God formed mankind in his image and bestowed upon us the gift of free will, granting us authority over the earth. To test our faith and love, he planted two trees in the middle of the Garden of Eden—the tree of life and the tree of knowledge of good and evil. As we enjoyed the bliss of our relationships with God and each other, we were free to eat from any tree except the latter. However, one of God's creations, a being who sought to be God himself, was filled with envy and rebellion. This being led a revolt against God but was defeated and cast out of heaven. In his hatred towards mankind, he tempted the first man and woman to eat from the forbidden tree, tricking them into believing they could become like God. Their disobedience brought about the fall of man and the loss of their authority to an evil taskmaster. In that moment, our world was plunged into chaos and darkness."

Rosie heard the distant clattering of a dinner cart being rolled down the hallway. Soon after, an orderly came in to serve Ethan's meal. The orderly raised an eyebrow at Rosie when he entered.

Rosie felt a natural break in the conversation. "Could I have some time to think and come back tomorrow to talk some more?"

"Of course." Ethan extended his hand. "It was an honour to meet you."

Rosie took his hand and felt an otherworldly warmth travel up her arm; it made her feel completely loved and accepted. The sensation was like being touched by liquid love, and it sparked a hunger within her.

"God really does love you, Rosie."

"Thank you, Ethan. I'll see you tomorrow."

With much to ponder, Rosie left the room and headed home.

Ethan watched as Rosie walked out, grateful for this second chance at life. Though he was excited about the prospect of speaking again with Rosie, he also felt a gentle prompting from the Holy Spirit within him to be gentle and compassionate. He sensed her deep hurt, brokenness, and lack of trust.

He picked up his journal from the bedside table and took a moment to reflect before writing down his thoughts. He couldn't help but envision a young child huddled in a dark hole. But his mind's eye was drawn to a radiant figure of light standing patiently at the entrance of the hole, waiting for the child. It was God the Father, extending His loving and comforting presence and giving her time to trust in Him. He wasn't going anywhere; to the Father, Rosie was worth waiting for.

Ethan considered himself nothing more than a servant of heaven, working with his Father to help Rosie see that she could abide in his love and power. It was the very purpose of humanity, at the heart of their ability to have faith in something greater than themselves.

As Rosie lay asleep that night, she dreamed herself standing in the middle of a beautiful field surrounded by wildflowers. Nearby stood a man, a man whom she sensed was named Yeshua. He was bald and had a dark beard that contrasted with his fair skin. Though he wasn't conventionally handsome, Rosie found him strangely compelling.

The wind blew softly through the trees, creating a sweet melody that seemed to harmonize with Yeshua's gentle voice. The rose-coloured light of dawn shone all around the field. In the distance lay mountains, and their colours made Rosie think of the cosmos.

Rosie took a few tentative steps towards Yeshua and stopped. She could faintly hear a song on the wind.

"Rosie," Yeshua began, speaking with a tenderness she'd never heard before. "I love you. Long ago, I dreamt of you and the thought of giving you life filled me with great joy. Two thousand years ago, you were the joy set before me, for which I endured the cross. All your life, I have been right here, pursuing you and wanting you to know who I am. If you will trust me with your life, and receive my love, you will learn a new way to live. Along that road, your stumbling steps will be healed. There will be challenges, yes, but you will never be alone, not even for a minute."

As he spoke, the music on the wind got louder, lending a beautiful tune to Yeshua's words. He walked closer to her, until they were only two feet apart. The sound of music grew stronger with every step.

"Rosie, this is my song of love towards you. Will you dance with me?" Yeshua reached out his hand towards her.

After a brief pause, Rosie stretched out her hand to take his. "Yes, I will." And there they danced until the stars came out; Rosie didn't want that dance to end.

As the first light of day began to illuminate the sky, Rosie's eyelids slowly parted and she was greeted by profound tranquillity and elation. She couldn't quite put the feeling into words, but it felt as though a heavy burden had been lifted from her shoulders and she was ready to take on the day with a clear and open mind.

Without any hesitation, she got up and made her way to her cedar hope chest, which contained all her most precious possessions. After a few minutes of searching through the contents, she finally found what she was looking for: her grandmother's Bible. It had been years since she had last opened it, but today felt like the perfect day to revisit the stories and teachings that had shaped her childhood.

She took the Bible to her favourite place to sit, a comfortable armchair positioned near the window, and carefully opened the book to the well-thumbed pages that recounted the story of Yeshua, the same stories that had captivated her as a young girl. The pages held notes in her beloved grandmother's handwriting, which is why Rosie hadn't had the heart to get rid of the book.

In previous years, Rosie had struggled to accept the stories as true, having never witnessed any tangible proof of God's power and love during childhood. Yet Rosie's heart yearned for a sign that would validate her belief in him and ease the pain of feeling misunderstood and rejected by those who were supposed to love her.

However, yesterday a miracle had taken place. Ethan, who had been dead, now lived. This experience offered Rosie the tangible proof she had always craved. Her heart swelled with joy and gratitude for the divine intervention. She knew the experience would help her overcome the stigma of being misunderstood and rejected.

As a child, she had felt so hurt and confused that she had stopped attending church after her grandmother's death. Now, as she read the Bible—and savoured some chocolate—a fresh fire to know God personally was sparked in her soul, drawing her towards him with renewed passion and faith.

EIGHT

The hospital gym was quiet and empty except for Arden, who was in the middle of a vigorous workout. He was taking out his anger on the boxing bag, hitting it with all his might. His shirt was soaked with sweat, his knuckles raw and bleeding under the tape, but he didn't seem to care or even notice.

Earlier that day, Ethan and Trent had been moved out of the ICU and were on the path to recovery. However, Aaron remained in critical condition, and Arden couldn't shake the feeling of helplessness that came with it.

As he punched the bag, memories of his own dark past resurfaced. He struggled to control his emotions.

Josh quietly entered the room and watched his friend from a distance. The sound of Arden's laboured breathing and the thuds of his fists hitting the bag echoed. Josh thought back to the beating Trent had suffered at Aaron's hands, as well as the suffering of Yeshua.

Despite his concerns, Josh couldn't help but marvel at the force and skill behind Arden's blows. It was clear he had years of training and experience, both in the ring and on the soccer field.

But as he watched, Josh couldn't help but wonder if there was more to Arden's backstory than he had revealed. His friend's actions during the park incident and his current display of power hinted at something much darker and more complex than Josh had ever imagined.

After a brief pause, Josh quietly crossed the gym and found a seat near Arden's workout area. As Josh settled down, he reached into his backpack and took out two energy drinks.

"What's going on, man?" he asked Arden. "Is everything okay?"

Arden turned to face Josh, his expression troubled. "I don't know. There's something eating me up inside, but I'm not sure I can talk about it."

Josh placed a reassuring hand on Arden's shoulder. "Hey, don't worry about it. You can tell me anything. We're friends. And we're here for each other no matter what. That's what our family's honour code is all about."

Arden looked at Josh, his eyes filled with uncertainty. "I don't know if I'm ready to share. It's something that might make you see me differently."

Josh smiled warmly. "Nothing can change the bond we share. We stand by each other no matter what comes our way. Our friendship isn't based on what we do or don't do, but on what has been done for us by God. Together, we are established in God's Son, Yeshua Christ."

When Arden spoke, his voice was troubled and deeply pensive. Josh could hear the frustration and confusion in it.

"Why is there so much pain and discord in the family, even among our brothers and sisters?" Arden said. "Why do we only seem able to hurt one another? Why does hate and anger so easily rise to the surface? People get angry over the smallest things. When will this feud ever end? What is the point of all this? Why is my past coming back to haunt me now? To be brutally honest, my conscience is confused and my heart deeply troubled. Would you still love me, Josh, even if I told you the brutal truth of who I was before joining the family of light?"

For a brief moment, Josh paused. "Arden, we all have a past. We've all done things that make us feel ashamed. But that's in the past. We are a new creation by faith in Yeshua. You're my brother, and nothing you've done will ever change that. I'll always stand by you, love you with Christ's love, and be there, no matter what you've done. No matter the cost."

Arden took a deep breath before coming clean. "I used to be an assassin for the rival family, responsible for poisoning our brothers and sisters. Taking their lives. Snuffing out their dreams, passions, and lives with a lie. I loathe the senselessness of that rivalry and the fact that so many people are unwittingly enslaved by harsh and dark masters. Josh, I confess to you that forgiving myself, and Aaron, is impossible in my own strength."

As Arden shared his burden, he sobbed uncontrollably. The weight of what he had done hung heavily and he wondered how he could stop living in the past, as they had been taught.

Josh, his confidant, listened intently. "Arden, are you still allowing your past to define your identity? Your identity should be found being a child of the Father of lights. Are your values and beliefs fully aligned with our family? Are you still trying to live according to your old habits, lifestyle, and thoughts? What gives your life worth? Is it the opinions of others or what God thinks about you?"

Josh gently turned Arden's body to face him, his eyes locking onto his brother's.

"Arden, you are Father Light's son. I, for one, am proud to be your brother. I'm loyal to the end. This life we're in is a journey of discovery in the family. You don't have to struggle alone."

Moved by his brother's words, Arden leaned in to embrace him, tears streaming down his face. The two men held each other, their bodies shaking with sobs—and as they wept, the presence of heaven's healing balm flowed around them, easing their pain and comforting their souls.

Although Father Light didn't answer every question, the brothers felt his presence helping to bear their grief and provide solace in their time of need.

Later that day, at 5:03 a.m., Aaron's monitor flatlined. In the spirit realm, Yeshua came to bring Aaron home to heaven for eternity. The brothers and sisters gathered around his bed, their hearts heavy with sorrow.

Tina, Trent, Ethan, Arden, Josh, and Ashley all stood together, united in their grief as they said goodbye to their beloved brother. Trent and Ethan were still connected to portable IV poles, but they didn't care.

The group prayed, asking for Aaron to come back to life, but the Lord assured them that it was his time to come home. And in heaven, the news of Aaron's arrival was greeted with joyous celebration, not sadness. For Aaron, it was the beginning of a new journey, one filled with light, love, and eternal peace.

At the hospital, though, the group gathered in a moment of silence, each lost in their own thoughts. The stillness of the air gave rise to a sombre mood that no one seemed eager to break.

Finally Trent spoke up, his voice soft but firm. "We are all here today to mourn the loss of our brother Aaron, and the potential of his life that was cut short. Though we grieve, we do not fear death, for we believe that through Yeshua God has defeated it. Our hope lies in the promise of eternal life beyond the grave. But what are we doing with the time we have been given? The world is full of people who are dying inside, desperate for hope, love, meaning, and everything that makes life worth living."

Trent paused as he looked around at his companions.

"As followers of the King, we are charged with sharing the message that all are welcome into his family. There is always room, and the price has already been paid for anyone's transfer. It is a gift we are called to unwrap and share with others every day."

He then turned to Ethan, who was sitting beside him.

"What did you learn from knowing Aaron, even for a brief time?" Trent asked.

Ethan took a deep breath. "I learned the importance of always being ready to share what we have been freely given, even in the midst of violent and bizarre circumstances. God has placed desires in everyone. They're woven into the very fabric of our beings. I also learned that extending grace and forgiveness to those who hurt us is never easy, but it's a vital part of our family's values. This experience has taught me to never take second chances for granted."

Trent nodded. "I experienced suffering with the Lord as I was beaten and thought I was about to die. He was right there with me. I experienced peace, excitement, and joy because I would see the Holy Trio face to face."

"I know what it means to love your enemies as Yeshua did." Tina met the eyes of her adopted brothers. "We loved this man, Aaron, into the Father's family. We forgave and showed undeserved mercy to a member of our rival family. Through this time of suffering, we have become more resilient."

There was a long pause, which Josh was the first to break. "I've learned that to honestly know another person is to know and understand their depths," he said. "I've seen firsthand the cost of giving and accepting grace in this world. I've also personally discovered a deeper trust in the Lord. He will lead me through every decision I make. Both inwardly and outwardly."

Arden was the last to speak. "I've learned from regret that I haven't embraced the fullness of my new identity in this new family. If I had, I could have shared with Aaron my similar experience. I now belong to the rival family he and I both fought so long and hard against."

Everyone stood together, shoulder to shoulder. The silence was one of honour, respect, and understanding that surpassed any words. One by one, they hugged each other, saluted their fallen brother, and left the room.

NINE

O ver the course of the next two weeks, Ethan busily got back to his regular life. He was discharged from the hospital and attended Aaron's small funeral before returning home. He now couldn't help but wonder why he had been given a second chance to live while Aaron hadn't. This question weighed heavily on him.

Seeking answers, he decided to talk to Father Light about it.

With a heavy heart, he pulled on his running clothes and laced up his shoes. He often went on runs to help him connect with his Father and clear his mind. Today, however, he had a feeling that running on the hard pavement wouldn't be enough to help him deal with the overwhelming sense of loss and sadness he felt.

Instead he decided to seek out one of the nature trails that wound their way through the city. Being surrounded by lush greenery and the sweet melodies of birds would help him find the solace and clarity he so desperately needed.

As Ethan pulled into the parking lot at the bluff, he noticed Trent's vehicle waiting for him. His friend was sporting a pair of shorts and bright red hoodie that stood out against the greenery. They embraced each other warmly, excited for the adventure ahead.

As they made their way towards the trailhead, they eagerly chatted about their plans for the day. When they finally started running, one followed closely behind the other.

Birdsong echoed through the woods while nimble squirrels chased each other high up in the branches. The ground beneath the men's feet was a mixture of dirt, rocks, and roots, creating a natural obstacle course. With each step, their hearts pumped faster and their breath became more laboured. It was an exhilarating experience.

The duo climbed to the top of a bluff that offered a view of the forest below. From there, the trail opened up into a clearing that overlooked the sprawling expanse of Lake Superior. The stunning panorama, with the warmth of the sun and gentle breeze, showcased the untamed beauty of nature.

As Trent sat under a moss-covered tree, enjoying the ambiance, a beautiful bluejay landed on the branch above him. The bird began singing a melodious tune, which made Trent burst into laughter.

"I think this is our cue to give God a sacrifice of praise and thanksgiving," he said, turning to Ethan. "Let's take turns and each say one thing for which we're thankful."

Trent took the lead and expressed his gratitude to God for giving him and Ethan more time. Ethan followed suit and shared that he felt blessed to be alive and surrounded by so much beauty.

The bluejay chirped as if to cheer them on.

"Thank you, Father, for creating that bluebird," Trent added.

Ethan smiled. "Thank you, God, for creating everything and sustaining life with your words."

A sparrow flew towards them and perched itself next to the bluejay.

"Thank you for your word and Son, Yeshua, who governs our lives."

"Thank you, Lord, for leading us down unfamiliar roads."

"Thank you, God, for your presence and love in our lives."

"Thank you, Father, to everyone who prepared Aaron's funeral."

"Thank you to the friends with whom we are blessed to have journeyed through life."

"Thank you for more time on the earth with you, God, the Holy Trio, our families, and friends."

At that moment, a robin arrived at the gathering. As time passed, the birds' music gelled into a beautiful combination of worship and gratitude. Trent and Ethan couldn't help but laugh, which frightened the birds and caused them to scatter into the boreal forest.

Afterward they sat in silence, comfortable with each other's company. Their souls leaned in to hear the Father's voice in the stillness.

An unknown amount of time passed as they each listened to the voice of the one they sought. Father Light's words brought renewed strength, courage, peace, and joy. Trent and Ethan wrote down the words they heard in small notepads they'd brought with them. They were filled with songs, scriptures, poems, key words, phrases, and even some doodles.

"I am with you," the voice said. "I will never leave you or forsake you. I have called you by name. You are mine. Beloved son, I am your strength, courage, joy, and song."

As the friends sat together, they felt wells of faith springing up within them. They spoke about the promises of God, praying aloud and in their hearts for those around them. They asked for all that God had in store for them and declared their faith in his word. They encouraged each other and built up their confidence in God, praying with conviction, passion, and compassion. Each knew how important it was to have a strong relationship with God the Father, God the Son, and the God the Holy Spirit, each being unique in personality and wholly unified.

During their time of prayer, certain moments evoked strong emotions. At times, the experience felt too profound and extraordinary to articulate in words. However, the Holy Trio heard their voices and granted them release from all their fears, calming the turbulent waters in their souls.

They prayed for each other as the Holy Spirit led, strengthening and encouraging one another in the faith. They shared images, spontaneous thoughts, longings of the heart, and scriptures that came to mind. The Holy Spirit rose up in power to break the enemy's yokes. This helped them to keep growing in their faith and strengthened their bond.

Ethan grinned widely, revelling in his joy.

Trent hugged his sweaty brother in the faith. "I see the Lord embracing you, saying, 'I love you, my son.'"

"I believe and receive that."

"Come on, let's race down the hill! The winner gets to bless the other with a meal!"

"You're on!"

The men raced down the hill, egging each other on for the privilege of getting to bless the other.

When they reached a grassy area near the parking lot, Ethan tackled Trent and knocked him over. Trent rolled across the grass, laughing as Ethan ran into the middle of the lot and performed a victory dance.

"I won!" Ethan exclaimed. "It's my turn to bless you!"

The friends' laughter brought a joy-filled smile to Yeshua's face in heaven's throne room.

"That's my brother!" he shouted in great delight.

Across town, Tina met with Rosie for coffee. The nurse was struggling to reconcile the world she knew with the fact of Ethan being alive again.

To help explain, Tina decided to share a personal story.

"Growing up, I saw people I loved deal with pain and physical health issues daily. It was difficult to see this. I also couldn't see any difference between the lives of believers in my church and those out in the world. In my twenties, I began to hear stories about God's love and redemptive power in the lives of others. Then I experienced firsthand his resurrection power. The new way I was able to live on a daily basis was a reminder that God had changed my life forever. The Lord asked me, 'Tina, do you trust my goodness? That my power is abundantly sufficient in any situation? That I have the strength to break your chains and destructive patterns? That I'm bringing new life to the dry bones of your lives and world? Will you trust that I am greater than your fear of not being enough? Trust me with every situation, circumstance, and care in your life. Let me lead you rather than look to external sources for guidance.' These questions challenged me to trust God in everything. I needed to put my trust in God's power, as he intended, and realize that my understanding of life and God wasn't entirely accurate. Meditating on his words, love, passion, and character changed my perspective."

Tina watched Rosie carefully. The woman seemed to listen very closely to what Tina had to say.

"I won't lie to you, Rosie," Tina continued. "Being in God's family isn't always sunshine, lollipops, and rainbows. There are hard days and painful moments. Understanding why difficult things happen can be a struggle. But beyond the tears and pain is the opportunity to experience the Lord's comfort, to get to know him who tasted death for us in a new way. In the depths of my life, God is abundantly sufficient. Faith in God stirs within us a declaration of what has yet to be seen—as if it already exists! You can pull heaven's reality into your earthbound life."

Tina took out a copy of the Bible and slid it across the table towards Rosie.

"This is for you… if you want to accept it."

Rosie picked up the book and began to skim its pages at random.

Tina pressed on. "As you read God's word, ask yourself, 'What is God's character and attitude? Seek to understand Father Light's heart of love. Then intimacy between you will begin to grow. Talk to the Lord about everything and take the time to listen. God wants this intimacy with you but gives you a choice about how deep you'll go with him."

Rosie had a lot to ponder. "Thank you, Tina."

"You're welcome, Rosie. I have one more bit of encouragement for you: God sees all of who you are, not just the external parts. He loves the whole you, the real you. Father Light is concerned with your inner world: your character, your heart, thoughts, perspective, values, convictions, emotions, and beliefs. They all shape how we live—at least, externally… how we relate to God and everything he created."

She paused for a moment, wanting to give the other women enough time to let this sink in.

"Always remember this: in our lives, faith is determined by the ideas and thoughts we choose to agree with," added Tina. "What you choose to listen to is a key part of the process. None of us can escape the influence of the unseen war raging even now."

At that moment, in the unseen realm, a battle raged for the kind of faith Tina had been speaking about. The two rival families had very different purposes for humanity. One focused on hate and sought to destroy God's image of humans on the earth. The other was zealous in its work to restore and establish God's original intent.

The evidence of this battle revealed itself in the swirl of human thought, in the mixed messages their brains constantly received, the ups and downs of their emotions. Humans often were given only a partial picture of what happened in the world and the lives of others, and so they made quick and lasting judgments based on the smallest of impressions. They only believed of others based on what they could see and understand based on previous experience.

But some had learned to see what could not be seen through natural eyes. Those who sought wisdom were present at the foundation of the world, dancing with delight at God's creation. Even now, they remembered God's intent in creating all things with purpose—to know, believe, and trust the Holy Trio: Father Light, the Son, and the Holy Spirit—with the intention that humans would have faith in the same power of God to create and sustain all life.

The father of lies and his cronies sought to steal, kill, and destroy all that had been created in God's image. They hated the very ones they ruled over and imprisoned in darkness. Having tricked the first humans into giving away their authority, they manipulated men and women by using their own desires to lure them away from God's heart.

Ultimately, this was the dark master Aaron had served.

In the end, by trusting in Yeshua, Aaron was transferred into God's family. He could never have earned this precious gift. He could gratefully receive it.

In Thunder Bay, the brothers and sisters of God's family sought the greater glory of God in and through their lives together. Amidst the test and trials, they endured by trusting in God. They looked out for one another, believing in God's word with a determination of purpose that all would arrive home in the end. The Holy Spirit bonded them, partly through their shared experiences of God's glory, mainly through his freely flowing love.

TEN

Eight and a half months later

Ronald Nelson, once known as Daredevil Deathgiver a lifetime ago, fumbled with his keys to his tiny one-room apartment. The man had skin as black as midnight, a long beard, and wore faded jeans, a green T-shirt, and a plaid long-sleeved shirt full of holes. His body odour and no-nonsense facial expression usually kept strangers at bay, which was the way he liked it. The haunting memories he harboured from his secret former life were constant companions, each one having its own voice to accuse him. At times, the memories caused his hands to shake, as they did now, reminding him of the money and lives he'd taken.

You're a scumbag. You're not worth living. We're coming for you. The time is coming for you to pay with your life. Death will arrive painfully and without warning. You belong to us.

Yet deep within his heart, Ronald had a longing he never expressed but secretly acknowledged: *There must be more to life than this. It can't be all I'm here for.* It was his heart's deepest cry.

When he tried again to open the door, he dropped his keys. On the third try, he stepped through the doorway and turned on the light. In the same motion, he grabbed the bottle on the table.

Empty. Bone dry. Just like the rest of the bottles and his life.

The negative thoughts and accusing voices continued their mantra. *What's the point of carrying on? Each day and night is the same as the last—dulling the pain with hard liquor, waking up who knows where, and finding some way to scrape together enough to cover the rent for this dump, living off the handouts and castoffs of others...*

The tension between Ronald's deep longings, the voices, and the memories threatened to tear him apart. Drinking was the only way he found anything remotely like rest, enabling him to temporarily silence his inner turmoil.

Glaring memories of Dallas, Brussels, and the desert flashed through his mind, just like they had done countless times. Not for the first time, he considered ending it all. He left that door open. He just needed a reason to keep going, some way to drown the pain he constantly felt.

He couldn't stay here.

Ronald left the apartment and went back out in the rain, trudging along the street that led to his favourite pub, Roxie's.

That's when he made a decision. If fate didn't stop him within the next thirty hours, he would end his life. He would do it at precisely 11:49 the next evening.

Less than a second later, a thought came to him.

Why wait? I could jump off a bridge, splash down into the water below, and no one would be the wiser. Who cares about me? Would anyone miss me or realize I'm gone?

Truth be told, Ronald didn't know whether his mom was dead or alive and hoped his old man was dead. Last he'd heard, the man was living in Texas taking part in a rehab program.

"They never work," Ronald muttered. "No program like that ever works. No one has any answers. Change is impossible; everyone stays the same. We humans only know brokenness. Anxiety, despair, and depression are our lot in life. What's the purpose in life for any of us?"

Yet Ronald still had certain secret, unexplained desires in his heart, although he had no visible evidence to show that there was anything more to life than what he'd seen, done, heard, and experienced.

"Tomorrow seems as good a day as any to die," he muttered to himself.

Passersby on the didn't hear and appeared to give him no second thought.

By this time, Ronald had arrived at Roxie's Roadhouse on Square Street. Roxie's was a low-end bar that made no attempt to hide the raw pain of its patron's broken lives. No one here hid their mess, but they built up walls to keep others out. There was a whole wall at the far end of the bar where graffiti artists could express themselves in any way. If you were offended by something on the wall, though, and said something about it to the staff, they would tell you to go to hell.

Ronald went to the bar and asked for a beer and double shot of whisky, then gave the bartender a ten and got some change back. Sometimes, but not always, he sat at the bar and watched whatever was on the TV screen. Tonight he decided to sit near the far end—in the corner, of course, because he never sat with his back to an open room.

Absentmindedly, he looked at the graffiti wall next to his table as took a swig of beer. What he saw caused him to spit it out his beer and laugh at the absurdity of what he saw. Someone had painted "God loves you" in fancy letters beside a man hanging on a cross.

Bitter pain filled him.

That's stupid, he said. *We all know that isn't true! Any God in control of so much chaos must have major temperament issues. Even more so than my old man... and he could give quite the whipping when angry and not remember anything he'd done the next day after sleeping it off...*

Ronald wiped his beard with a napkin and downed the whisky. Then he slugged his beer as if it were nothing and abruptly ordered one more shot of whisky before heading out the door.

With that, he decided that he'd had enough of this place for today. He'd go buy a bottle of hard liquor and find a dry place outside to drink the night away.

That night, the Holy Trio heard Ronald's challenge and the cry of his heart. They'd been preparing for a long time and were about to rock his world with their powerful love. Ronald had just dared them to stop him from ending his life, and they would. Beyond that, they would give him a new reason, perspective, and way to live. He would be given the choice to receive and walk in their priceless gift: a new life.

Two hours later, Ronald sat with a bottle of gold-coloured hard liquor underneath a tree in the nearby park. At least the rain had stopped. He'd drunk a quarter of the bottle and was about to take another swig when a flashback came upon him. There was no stopping it.

Of everyone who could have been hit, it ought to have been him. But Connie, their squad medic, had seen the sniper aiming, then shoved him out of the way and took the bullet for him. Always chipper and bright, even in this wartorn country, Connie gasped for breath as she lay dying on the ground.

Ronald held a clean rag to the wound in her shoulder as Richie called in for an immediate evacuation. They were surrounded and had men down and needed air cover—but looking down at Connie, Ronald knew it wouldn't come fast enough. She knew it, too; he could see it in her eyes.

But he could also see a peace deep inside her. He couldn't fathom where it came from.

"Ronald..." She struggled to speak through the agony. "This wasn't your fault... I made the choice to save your life—"

She began to cough and hacked up a stream of blood.

"Don't try to talk, Connie. Save it! Tell me later."

"No, Ronald, I'm not going to make it. Listen to me... I need to tell you why I took that bullet." Connie took a quick breath. "Yeshua gave his life for us, so we would know that God gave us life. He showed me that you need him, but you've been running. He's relentless. He won't give up on you. He wants you to know he's good, Ronald... that he loves you."

Connie coughed again, but she didn't seem to notice the pain anymore. Her eyes took on a strange look, as if she was looking into heaven itself.

"Ronald, you are special to the Father. He has a good plan for your life. He made you to be his, alone. That's why nothing else ever satisfies you. And I love you like Yeshua."

As these words came out of her mouth, she breathed her last. Then she was gone. The only light Ronald had known in this life... was gone. Completely extinguished—forever.

Under the tree in the park, Ronald roared with rage over his loss.

"Why did she have to die instead of me, you idiot!" he demanded, shaking a fist towards the sky. "I deserved the bullet, not her! She was too good to die the way she did."

Hot, agonized tears rolled down his face as he opened the whisky bottle and chugged half the remaining liquor before passing out on the cold, hard ground.

In the wee hours of the morning, Ronald was awakened by a powerful flashlight shining in his face.

"You son of a bitch!" shouted a harsh voice. It sounded just like the one in his own head.

"You don't deserve to live!"

"You're a worthless piece of shit and a mama's boy!"

"You can't do anything worthwhile!"

"No one loves or cares about you!"

They started hitting and kicking him. On the face, the stomach, anywhere and everywhere they could. All the while they called him every bad name he'd ever been called. It reminded him of all the evil he'd done. All the people he'd killed in the line of duty.

One of the men poured the rest of the liquor over his head and smashed the bottle on the tree behind him, showering Ronald with the glass.

They're going to kill me, he consoled himself. Might as well get it over with. Hurry up and kill me, whoever you are.

Suddenly, a light more potent than the sun shone down all around them; the men screamed and hollered.

"Get away from us!"

"We don't want anything to do with you!"

As they started to run away, they shouted back at Ronald: "This isn't over yet! You still belong to our master…"

Stunned and bewildered, Ronald forced himself to his feet. The brilliant light was gone, although it felt like he was still surrounded by many people, but this time they were helping him to his feet, helping him remain steady.

I can't stay here, he thought. *Whoever those guys were, they might be back.*

"We'll take you to a safe place and watch over you," a voice spoke, almost audible. *"We'll keep you concealed from prying eyes until our man comes."*

Dazed, Ronald allowed the unseen and possibly imaginary beings to lead him away from the park. He couldn't have seen where he was going even if he wanted to. But it didn't matter; in less than a day, he would be a dead man. That much he knew.

Caterpillar Journey

Yum, milkweed!

Eating

Green and gold cocoon

Green and black cocoon

Liquefied

Emerged

Drying

Gathering strength

Ready to fly

ELEVEN

Trent opened his eyes first thing in the morning, full of joy and anticipation for the day ahead. He looked out the window and took in the sky, painted with purple, pink, and blue, all amazingly reflecting the light of the rising sun. Wondrously, the light gradually dispelled the darkness. The sun's brilliant light spoke of God's goodness and faithfulness. The birds joined in the chorus of praise. It was a new day for all to know the Father personally, experiencing his grace and mercy anew.

"Morning, Papa," Trent said. "I love you! Who do we get to love on today?" And he already knew the answer. "Of course, that will be everyone you put in front of me!"

That's when Trent heard Father Light speak directly to his heart.

"I have someone extra special I want to love today. His name is Ronald, and he's been hurt. I need you to take him to the hospital and stay with him. I'll lead you right to him."

Immediately, Trent called Tina, who would soon be going to work at the same café as him.

She picked up sleepily on the second ring. "Hello?"

"Hi Tina, it's Trent. Could you take my seven to three shift today? Father Light has given me a very specific loving assignment, and that takes priority."

"Of course, Trent!"

"Pray for him. His name is Ronald. And if the Holy Spirit gives you anything about him, send me a message."

"Go love on Ronald with Father Light's heart of gold. You're famous for that! If you need anything else, just let me know." She paused. "By the way, do you want me to meet you somewhere after work?"

"If you have peace about it, sure! In that case, shoot me a message."

"All right! Blessings in Yeshua's name."

"Blessings, sister. Ciao for now!"

Trent hurried to prepare for what promised to be a big day with Father Light, full of adventure and his supernatural love.

Some time later, after getting ready for his assignment, Trent got into his vehicle with his ever-present backpack. Stilling his heart to hear from the Holy Spirit, he asked where to go.

"Go to the Living Waterhole. My servants are guarding Ronald there."

The Living Waterhole was an unusual young people's church that Trent and his friends had started, a place where people young and old could meet God. Frankly, it was quite unconventional and messy, different from the average church and full of Father Light's heart. From floor to ceiling, it was full of the Lord's presence. Everyone was welcome, and all who encountered the Lord there were never the same.

It was Wednesday, though, and no one was around this early. Trent started the engine and headed to the waterfront district.

"Thank you, dear Lord, for your wonderful love and goodness," he prayed while driving. "Thank you, God, for your mercy and grace that are new every morning. I praise you, for I am fearfully and wonderfully made. Thank you, Father Light, for your loving-kindness. I'm thankful to be your son and precious in your sight. Thank you for Ronald, and your heart of love towards him. Open his eyes to see and know you, Lord. I ask for your grace and mercy on his life. Love on Ronald, Lord! He needs you, not me. I get out of the way and ask you, God, to have your way in Ronald's life. Show him the revelation of his value in your eyes, Yeshua. Value worth dying for. Unravel the lies and replace them with truth. Change Ronald from the inside out through close relationship with you, God, so he would know by personal experience your love and power!"

The whole way, Trent praised and thanked the Lord for his wonderful love and goodness. He praised him for Ronald and God's great love, grace, and mercy. He prayed with the Holy Spirit and gave a joyful noise to the Lord, who delighted in him who called him a son. Trent knew that his acceptance came from Father Light, not from man.

In return, Father Light reminded Trent that his confidence, peace, and strength were in him alone. He didn't have to strive. He lived in a place of victory because of Yeshua's death on the cross.

"I love you, Trent, so much more than you know. Keep going, my son! Everyone at home in heaven is cheering you on."

Pulling up at the Living Waterhole, Trent immediately spotted Ronald slumped next to the front door. The man was covered in dirt and blood. The shards of glass on his worn jacket sparkled in the dawn light.

Ronald's skin was as black as the midnight skies Trent loved to watch, and the Father's love and compassion instantly sprang up inside him as he walked over to the front door and gently shook Ronald's shoulder.

"Ronald. Ronald…"

To Ronald, the voice and touch were strange. Foreign. Whoever this man was, he spoke in a strong Scottish accent. The voice was full of something tender and gentle Ronald hadn't heard before.

He groaned and tried to open his eyes, but they were sealed shut.

"I can't open my eyes," Ronald muttered. "What do you want, buster? Come to finish the job you started?"

"I want to take you to the hospital to get you checked out. First, though, let's get you cleaned up a bit."

That's weird, Ronald thought. *Why would anyone want to take me to the hospital? I hope he drops me off and I never hear from him again.*

Ronald heard a backpack unzip and something being taken out of it. Soon a wet towel was being wiped against his face, first one eye and then the other.

He finally opened his eyes to gaze upon this stranger who had said he was willing to help. The man crouching in front of him had blue eyes that seemed to shine from within. Something about them made Ronald feel like he was face-to-face with his maker.

The stranger was also about the same age as Ronald, and this gave him the courage to speak his mind.

"Where the hell have you been?" Ronald began in a loud voice, verging on a shout. He left no time for the stranger to answer. "What the heck were you thinking when you made this place? Why on earth did you make me this way? Why'd Connie have to die? Where in the hell did that flash of light come from that saved me last night? Why in the hell would you bother saving me anyway? The light in your eyes... where's that light been on the earth? Why'd my old man drink? Why'd he beat me? Why'd my mom run away and leave me with him? Why am I overwhelmed with fear, guilt, anxiety, anger, and rage every day? Why is nothing working out like I wanted it to? Why do I hate the man in the mirror?"

With that, he let out a scream that overflowed with rage.

When the scream finally petered out, the stranger in front of him did the last thing Ronald would have expected; he started to sing! His voice was clear, confident, bold, and full of love.

"You are my child; I love you," he began. "I made you in my image; I love you. I cherish you; I love you. I called you from your mother's womb as my own! I created you to be wild and free in your relationship with me. I gave my life for you to know me! I know all that you've done and all you've gone through. I love you, my lost son! I invited you to come home to me because you belong to me! I want to love you in a way you have never known. I've paid the price for your life to belong to me. Nevertheless, I freely give you the choice to be with me, or not. You are free to trust me, or not. Please, let me show you who you really are. My purposes and thoughts towards you are good. I desire for you to know me as I truly am. The way is through my Son, Yeshua Christ! The door home means turning from sin and back to me, turning from your own way of defining right and wrong. My power and divine nature are evident across the whole earth."

By the song's end, Ronald started to break down and cry. It was ugly and messy.

The stranger reached over to him and gave him a bear hug, simply holding him until Ronald was ready to let go.

"Who are you, man?" Ronald asked through his tears.

"I'm a Christian."

"What's your name?"

"Trent. Now, let's get you to the hospital. Are you hungry? I've got some fruit and peanut butter sandwiches in my bag. My vehicle is right over there. Can you stand and walk, Ronald?"

Ronald was shocked that Trent knew his name without ever having been introduced to him. Perhaps there had been some truth in the man's song after all.

Immediately, doubt rushed in. *No way, man. It can't be true. What about all the pain and power of the darkness?*

But another voice inside him fought back. *Shut up, whoever you are! I don't want to hear it right now.*

Trent helped Ronald to his feet, and together they walked over to the car by the side of the road. When Ronald had climbed inside, he realized how hungry he was; he couldn't remember the last decent meal he'd had.

"I'm hungry," he told Trent.

"Hi, hungry!" Trent had a big, goofy grin on his face. "Would you like peanut butter and jam, peanut butter and banana, or both?"

Ronald answered without a moment's hesitation. "Both."

Trent reached into his bag and brought out the sandwiches, an apple, and a bottle of water. The simple gesture brought tears to Ronald's eyes. "Thank you!"

"I love you, man. Now, let's go." Trent repacked his bag and put it in the backseat. He then started the car and they drove off.

Father Light, Yeshua, and the Holy Spirit were excited for this long-awaited meeting between Ronald and Trent. They'd been dreaming about Ronald knowing their love since the foundation of the world! But because they loved him, they were patient and kind to offer him friendship and a close relationship. They wouldn't force themselves on him. They were willing to do this on his terms.

Yet there was tension in the air from the great war for each human's trust.

Ronald and Trent walked up to the ER check-in desk. As they did, the Holy Spirit whispered to Trent about the young lady behind the desk.

"Her back has been hurting for five days straight. I want to heal her back because I love her. She is precious in my eyes, worthy of the blood of Yeshua. She's worried about being unable to provide for her family of four children. Give her the fifty-dollar bill in your wallet and pray for her back. I want to radically bless her."

"Hello," the nurse said. "How can I help you?"

"Hi! My friend here was beaten up last night, and we'd like to get him checked out." Trent smiled at her. "I hear that you have a problem with your back, and Yeshua wants to heal you. Can I see your hand, please?"

"What? Who told you that I have a problem with my back? It's been killing me for five days… well, okay. I guess you can. Right here?"

"Yes, right here, right now! God wants to heal your back because he loves you!" Trent took her hand and began to pray. "Father Light, in Yeshua's name, I ask for a new back! I pray that all the pain would go in the name of Yeshua! New discs and muscle tissue are knitting together right at the source of the problem, in Yeshua's name!" He opened his eyes. "Check it."

The nurse bent over behind the desk and shrieked! "What the heck? How are you… and what did you do? It's all better now! I feel no pain whatsoever…"

"I'm a Christian! God loves you so much that he wants to bless you!" Trent pulled out his wallet and retrieved a fifty-dollar bill. "Yeshua's Holy Spirit lives inside me, and he is the one who healed your back! He's asked me to give you this to help feed your family."

With that, the girl burst into tears.

Ronald was stunned; he'd never seen or heard anything like this before. He sort of wanted to know more about this Yeshua, but the voices in his head were shouting him down.

"No! It's not true. God doesn't love you. There's no one named Yeshua. Don't listen to him! He's lying."

The voice got so loud that it became impossible to hear what Trent and the nurse were saying to each other.

"I can't hear anything," Ronald exclaimed.

Trent put his hand on the man's shoulder and commanded, "In the name of Yeshua, let Ronald go!"

Immediately, Ronald could hear again.

"Wow! Weird. How did you do that, man?" Ronald started to freak out and got very disoriented. "What the hell is going on?"

Ronald lost complete control of himself, then turned around and ran out the door through which he had calmy walked just five minutes earlier. Except this time he sprinted straight through the glass, shattering it.

The next thing Ronald knew, he was running across the highway eleven blocks away. He darted right in front of a truck and barely missed getting hit. He smacked down hard on the pavement, losing consciousness.

Trent looked at the man-sized hole in the glass. *What now, Lord?* He turned back to the nurse, who looked totally shocked and terrified.

"Don't be afraid. I'll help pay for the broken glass," he said as she excused herself to get some water.

In the distance, Trent heard sirens. The Holy Spirit spoke to him with intensity, *"I need you and my other children to pray for Ronald! The fight is on for his life, like never before. He almost got hit by a truck on the highway. The enemy's camp is plotting to take his life before my love and power can be revealed to him. They've been tearing him apart from the inside his whole life. Only my perfect love can heal those wounds. I love Ronald as he is, but I don't want to leave him that way. I want to make whole the broken pieces of Ronald's identity, for it has been crushed while living in the enemy's bondage."*

Immediately, Trent pulled out his phone and sent emergency prayer messages to his prayer warriors near and far.

SOS, he typed. *Fight for the life of a lost friend named Ronald. He's been hurt, condition unknown. Papa sent me to find him. Remember, we fight for victory. Declare fullness of life in Yeshua's name and God's love, power, and authority!*

To Tina, he added a second message: *Please join me for prayer after work this afternoon at the hospital. This is an all-out war. Only our Lord Yeshua can rescue Ronald. Bring your guitar. Let's worship and sing praises to our Lord and King.*

Everyone who received his emergency message began to pray in faith, asking for Ronald to receive the fullness of new life in Yeshua. His goodness would cause Ronald to turn back to the Creator before it was too late. He needed to personally know and experience the passionate love of God, finding faith in his power.

In heaven, Father Light had one of his daughters on his ample lap. He held her tenderly in his arms.

"Father Light," she asked, "why do bad things happen?"

"My dear daughter, people must be free to choose whether they want to be with me. I don't force myself on them. They must have the option to decline my invitation, but that's when people feel a deep pain from lack. They don't always recognize or admit that this comes from not knowing me as I am. People often don't know their own quality. In their confusion, they take delight in created things, all the while knowing instinctively that they were made for love and to be loved. Their efforts can bring a temporary comfort, but when the feeling disappears they return to their search. I am the only one who can ever fully satisfy their hunger for love.

"On top of that, I have given mankind authority over the earth, but they in turn gave that authority to the enemy of their own souls. He's very jealous of my love for each one man and woman, but everything is made right when my children allow me to direct their choices in life, surrendering their lives to me. I have compassion for every person I created, but they believe lies about themselves, others, the purpose of life, and who I am. I desire to set everyone free to live in my love. This becomes possible when they are confident in me and my power to reconcile all things through my Son Yeshua."

Tears rose in his eyes as he became very sad.

"My stubborn children, why don't you trust me? If only you would dare to believe that what we've done is enough for you. The price we paid reveals how much we value each of you.

Even amidst pain, despair, and brokenness, our love for you is stronger. We see to the depths of your souls."

He looked down at his beautiful daughter.

"Daughter, won't you dare to trust me even more, believing in my word and treasuring it? Dare to stand in the power and authority that Yeshua's death and resurrection have given you—not for your own purposes, but for mine. Humbly serve others and bring my whole family home. Will you dare to live fully as a new creation, which my Son Yeshua died for you to have? Let go of your old, ragged way of doing things. Your former identity has been forever deprived of its power over you, unless you cling to it and refuse to let go. Will you let it go and open your hands to receive all that I have for you?"

TWELVE

The Holy Trio were very aware of the source of each and every pain eating Ronald up inside, including a particularly hard day he'd endured as a child.

While in the hospital, Ronald relived that pain in his dreams.

"Westly Ronald, you're a lazy good-for-nothing! Come back here with those cookies! I hate you, stupid boy!"

His mom shouted at him as he ran down the hall with a stolen cookie in each hand, and one in his mouth. He ran out the back door into the cornfield. He'd come back later, after she'd calmed down and forgotten about the cookies.

Hours later, when it was nearly dark, Westly returned home from playing in the creek past the field. He was covered in wet and dry mud from head to toe. There were no lights on and the house was quiet. He stepped into the kitchen and his heart told him the truth: his mom was gone.

She finally left the old man without me, *he thought,* leaving me to face his drunk rages and beatings alone. Fine then. I don't need her. I don't need anyone.

Something deep inside told him otherwise, but Westly ignored it and turned on the light. He grabbed a can of beans from the cupboard he'd hidden in hours earlier, then picked up a pot. He dumped the contents of the can and placed it on the stove.

He would show them. He'd make himself into a self-made man who didn't need anyone. He'd show the world that he was a man of steel.

For all his tough self-talk, though, Ronald was only an eight-year-old black boy whose tears ran down his cheeks after losing his mom. It was the only time he would ever allow himself to cry.

In the dream, however, the memory didn't play out the way Ronald remembered it. Something different happened this time.

A stranger bent down in front of the boy. Suddenly, they were both kneeling in the mud and rain fell all around them. To Ronald's surprise, the stranger embraced him and held him close.

Then the man spoke. "I have always been with you. You have never had to go through anything alone. I am intimately acquainted with pain and suffering."

Ronald opened his eyes and looked around him. Wherever he was, it was very dark. Was this the hospital? Creatures from his worst nightmares appeared around his bed—huge, hairy, scaly, bloody, and angry. They tied him down with a tight chain and began to beat him.

Suddenly, there was a blur of light. Then a second light! And a third! Whatever the lights were, they were blinding, and they almost seemed as though they were physically tormenting the hideous creatures around him.

"Send reinforcements!"

"They're on their way! We need more prayer cover! Rebuke them in Yeshua's name! Rebuke them! His is the name above every other name!"

Trent sat in the hospital room at Ronald's bedside. Beep-beep-beep. He listened to the sound of machines Ronald was connected to.

"Rebuke them in Yeshua's name! Rebuke them!"

"The Lord rebukes you in Yeshua's name!" Trent suddenly prayed. "Get your hands off him! I rebuke your plans and purposes for Ronald's life to end in death, for the Lord's plans are only for hope and good. Yeshua, my God and King, has defeated you, Satan! I will not allow you to take the life of this man, in Yeshua's name! His life has been bought and ransomed by the blood of Yeshua Christ!"

"Keep going! We need more covering of prayer!"

Tina walked down the hallway of the hospital with her guitar case in hand, headed for the intensive care unit, where Trent had told her to meet him. She suddenly felt a chill travel down her spine and instantly knew its meaning.

"Satan, I have put my hope, confidence, and trust in Yeshua Christ. I now break my agreement with you," she prayed. "Go away in Yeshua's name!"

With two takeout coffees in hand, she double-timed it to the ICU. Something told her to hurry, for time was short. As Trent had told them all by text, this was an all-out war for their lost brother whom Father Light wanted to redeem. As a daughter of the Most High God, she was to destroy all vestiges of hell on earth while she was here. She could do this only because of the complete victory Yeshua had won by dying on a cross and being raised back to life by the Holy Spirit's power.

"Lord, send your angel warriors straight from heaven to fight for your lost son," she prayed as she hurried through the corridor. "Set him completely free for your honour and glory,

Lord God! Let your holy name be praised throughout the whole earth!"

When Tina got to the nurses' station, she explained to the attendant that she was there to see Ronald.

"What room is he in?" Tina asked.

The nurse pointed down the hall. "He's in ICU room number three. The doctors say there ain't much hope for him, almost getting hit by a transport and all."

"In the name of Yeshua, Ronald will live," Tina insisted. "I declare life, hope, and healing over him through the precious blood of Yeshua. Ronald *will* see and declare the glory of God! He will be a living testimony of God's love, power, and goodness as God does a mighty new work."

She noticed that the nurse was looking at her oddly.

"Whether you believe it or not, ma'am, God does love you. He made you to love and be loved by him. To him, you're worth dying for! I can personally testify that living in a love relationship with our Creator God changes everything. It all begins when we choose to put our trust in Yeshua, who died in our place so we could be reconciled back to God and one another…"

From the dark place in which he found himself, Ronald saw more lights enter and join valiantly in the fight against the monsters of the dark. When he realized these lights were fighting for his life, he started to cry. They were fighting *for him.* The passion and courage with which they engaged in battle gave Ronald hope that Yeshua, whoever he was, was on his side, fighting on his behalf. A desire to meet him face to face began to form deep within him.

The hairy creature next to him kicked him in the head and Ronald passed out again.

When Tina walked into room three, she saw Trent standing in the middle of the room, praying and declaring victory in the name of Yeshua Christ.

"Hi Trent!"

He turned to look at her. "Thanks for coming, sister!"

"Any time, brother." She held up her guitar case. "I brought my guitar, like you asked. Why don't we start singing a new song of the Father's heart?"

Trent broke into a grin. "Great idea! Love it! Let's rock it!"

Tina got out her red guitar and together they started to sing lyrics that spoke the Father's heart over the man in the hospital bed. Trent turned on his cell phone's recorder so they could play it back for Ronald when he woke up.

Together they asked the Holy Spirit to help them sing a new song in unison over their brother. Gladly he complied with their request, and together they began to sing a beautiful song.

> There is a love that's deeper than the ocean,
> Stronger than the mountains,
> Steadfast, inclusive, and compassionate.
> One who hears the cries of those who are
> hurting
> Is coming near the humble and broken-
> hearted
> With pure love that heals all wounds and
> scars.
> Be not afraid, for you are loved beyond
> measure
> By our Creator and perfect Papa.
> He invites us all, "Come as you are,"

Rejecting none who call out to him for help.
These are the ones who dare to trust his
goodness,
Even in a world of chaos.
There is one who loves you more than you
know.
God died as a man for you to be freed from
sorrow.
You are loved, loved, ooooooo!
Loved by a good God who made all things!
His thoughts towards you outnumber the
grains of sand.
He holds the fabric of life in his hand!
His name is Yeshua! Yeshua!
Papa formed you in your mama's womb,
He gave you life and created you for himself,
Desiring to be with you always
As your closest friend.
Yeshua died for you, Ronald.
He died for you to receive a fresh start with
God,
To be made right before him by faith in
Yeshua!
Meet the Father who dreamed of you
Before the beginning of time!
Be not afraid! He loves you!
Be not afraid! God loves you!
Your life is in his hands!
Yeshua is the way, the truth, and the life.
No one comes to the Father except by him!
We were created for so much more,
To discover daily this wondrous love.

Ronald's phone suddenly began to vibrate, catching Tina's attention from the bedside where it had been placed. Even though the glass was broken, she could see that the incoming call was coming from *T. Challenge*. The area code was unfamiliar area.

The Holy Spirit prompted her to answer it. "Hello?"

"Hello. Who's this?" said a man's voice on the other end of the line. "Where is Ronald? I want to speak with him please."

"I'd love to do that, sir, but he can't talk right now. He's in the ICU here in the Thunder Bay hospital. My name is Tina. God sent my friend Trent to find him this morning."

There was a brief pause.

"I'm Ralph," the man said. "Thank you for letting me know about my son being in the hospital. You and Trent are a godsend!"

"You're Ronald's dad?" Tina replied, sounding elated. "This is so exciting! Can you come up to see him? Do you need any help getting here?"

"Sadly, I can't come just yet. I'm down in Texas for a year-long Teen Challenge program. And I can't leave early without quitting. I'll need to pray and ask the Lord what to do."

"Let's exchange phone numbers so we can keep in contact. I'll need to update you on his condition."

Once they'd exchanged numbers, including Trent's, the man thanked her again and agreed to pray alongside them for his son's healing.

"I'll ask my brothers down here to pray as well," Ralph said. "Can I speak to my son?"

"Sure you can. Just one moment." Tina held the phone up to Ronald's ear. "Go ahead!"

"I'm so sorry, son. I'm so very sorry, Ronald, for everything I put you through…"

Tina heard Ralph start to cry on the other end of the line.

"I'm so very sorry, Ronald, for everything I put you through…"

From the darkness, Ronald heard his old man talking and apologizing. The words sounded foreign to be coming from his dad. They sounded sincere, but the pain of bitterness was once again trying to grab hold of him. The prickly creature at Ronald's left shoulder bit into his arm. With the bite, his whole being felt dead and heavy.

"We're starting to lose him! We need the commander King to show up!"

The dark creatures began to shriek. *"No! We won't let you have him! Hold them off! Don't let those bastards beat you!"*

Suddenly, it was as though the sun itself walked into the room, only ten times brighter. Life itself seemed to radiate off this new arrival. Ronald heard the dark ones shriek.

"Who are you?" Ronald called out. He held up his hand to shield his eyes in a futile attempt to see the man who radiated light.

"I am Yeshua, King of kings and Lord of Lords! Son of God and Savior to all who put their faith and trust in me!"

THIRTEEN

Trent heard knocking at the hospital room door, and when he opened it he recognized the woman standing in front of him. It was the young nurse from the ER check-in desk, the one whose injured back the Lord had used him to heal that morning.

"Can I come in?" she asked.

Trent smiled. "Of course you can!"

"Thank you," the woman said as she stepped inside. "My name is Bella. Tell me, why do you believe in Yeshua? Why did you say all those things downstairs this morning? I've been wondering about it all day."

Father Light spoke to Trent through the Holy Spirit: *"I want you to share how my love has changed your life. Tell her that I've rescued you from yourself. You were always meant to be my son. Share with my daughter how I have Fathered you.*

"Bella, it's because of Yeshua who lives inside me that you have been healed," Trent explained. "I once was very lost, but now I've been found. It's on my heart to share with you the truth about him and what he's done in my life. It's a marvellous story of God's passionate love. All I ask is that you listen with an open heart, as parts of this may sound too good to be true…"

Ronald blinked. Yeshua, who had knelt next to him, no longer shone brighter than the sun. He looked like any man and was dressed in jeans and a long-sleeved plaid shirt. Yet there was an air of authority and otherworldliness about him, a passion and calm look in his eyes that said "You can trust me."

"Ronald, you have a choice to make here and now," Yeshua said. "You can stay with them and go eternally to be with their kind, apart from me. Or you can come with me, give me your life, and I will give you mine. Then you would have the life you were created for. No matter what you choose, I will always love you. But I am the only way you can ever be made right before my Father. Together, we dreamed and made you to love and be loved by us. We love you enough to give you the choice, Ronald. So do you want to be with us in life-giving intimacy for eternity? The choice is yours today. Who will you trust with your life? Will you turn from your own ways back to the God who made you? For the kingdom of heaven is at hand."

Ronald's mind went back in time to remember a conversation he'd once had with Connie before her death.

"Ronald, one day you're going to have to make a choice," she had told him. "The choice to trust God or not. Either way, you're going to have to live with what will happen."

He'd laughed it off at the time. Now he wasn't so sure of himself.

Ronald thought back over his life and the way he had lived. He'd really messed things up, trying to blame others for the consequences of his actions, beliefs, emotions, and thoughts. Even amidst this mess, though, Yeshua was offering him a new life in exchange for the old one. It seemed like a terrible trade for Yeshua.

He must see something in me that's worth more than I realize, thought Ronald. *I have no idea what that could be.*

Yeshua must really have meant what he'd said about loving him. No way could he have ever repaid such a wonderful gift of a new life. Nor had Ronald ever done anything to have warranted anyone dying for him.

The creatures around Ronald continued to shake, repulsed by Yeshua's very presence. That spoke volumes to Ronald as to this man's power and authority.

With his choice finally made, Ronald reached up with his hand towards Yeshua. Instantly the chains that had been holding him began to fall away.

He took Yeshua's hand in his.

"I trust you with my life, Yeshua, the Son of God."

The two held hands, and in a moment everything around him flashed the brightest white.

When Ronald opened his eyes, he found himself awake in the hospital bed. He had the sense that everything had changed and his life would never be the same.

Ronald looked around and saw Trent, as well as the young nurse from the ER and a second woman he'd never met before.

The first words out of his mouth were profound: "I believe in Yeshua. Please tell me more about him!"

Unexpectedly, Trent and the other woman began to tear up.

"Hallelujah!" Trent exclaimed. "Praise the Lord, for he is faithful and merciful! His love endures forever! Welcome to the family, friend. Today, this moment, is being celebrated in heaven because you have come home to the Father."

"I want to hear more about Yeshua, too," the nurse piped up. "I want to cry and belong with you all."

Her heart was open and desperately hungry for more in life. Bella had been searching for a long time for something real, something firm to build her life upon.

"When God made the world, he made us for himself, for us to live in perfect intimacy with him," Trent explained. "He loved us so much that he gave mankind a choice of whether to be with him, of whether to trust and obey him. The first human couple chose not to obey God and doubted his love and care for them. As mankind, our relationship with God became fractured with this deep wrestling over key questions. 'Does God love me? Can I trust that he is good?' Yeshua came and died so our sins could be covered by his blood and grace, so we could become the righteousness of God, being made right with him as if we were spotless and had never eaten from the tree in the garden. By eating once from this specific tree, we were able to determine for ourselves that which is good and evil. This creates conflict, with our 'good' clashing with other people's beliefs about what's 'good.' Instead we were designed to understand good and evil in the context of a relationship with the Holy Trio, who made us in their image—Father Light, Yeshua, and Holy Spirit. In wisdom, they created the earth from its foundation. We discover this wisdom when we humble ourselves before our Creator and ask him to be our teacher.

"But when our disobedience and distrust of God created a great gulf, there was no bridge for us to cross. Nor was it possible for us to create one because we are imperfect, not strong enough to make one that will last. Because Father, Son, and Spirit love us so much, though, desiring relationship with all people, Yeshua came and lived on the earth as a man in right relationship with Father Light through the Spirit. He was able to live in complete obedience out of perfect intimacy with Father Light through the Holy Spirit who lived inside of him. Yeshua died a gruesome death on a cross and took everything wrong in the world onto himself. That way, the dark influences on our lives could be forever cut off in the power and authority of his name. His death also created an opportunity for us to be remade as we were meant to be.

"Three days later, the Holy Spirit rose Yeshua from the dead to prove that God's power was at work in all this. When we put our hope, faith, and trust in Yeshua Christ, everything changes. A person spiritually dies and is raised to new life. His Spirit comes to make a home inside of us forever. We embark on a journey of becoming like Yeshua by walking in humble relationship with him. No believer in Christ gets everything right all the time, but it's Christ inside us that is the hope of glory! He's the one who healed you today, Bella, because of his wonderful love for you. There are no strings attached! We can't do anything to earn God's love."

Bella was having a hard time understanding all this.

"Where was that tree?" Bella asked. "What was it like in the beginning before we ate this fruit? Why did God make us? Please help me understand better."

The young woman Ronald had never met before began to share.

"The unseen God made and crafted the world through his word. Even before he began to shape everything from nothing and water, he was thinking and dreaming about us all. Like a master composer, he built and built and built to the crown of creation: man and woman. We were created to be in his family, to represent his character and heart on the earth. He made a beautiful garden and we walked together within it in perfect harmony. There was harmony and unity in our relationship with our Father and Maker.

"God wanted us to choose to have a relationship with him for ourselves, rather than force us, which is what gets depicted in many books, movies, and TV shows. In this life, many people are forced to be with people they don't love. By love, I mean genuinely caring for someone enough that you'd be willing to put their needs and interests before your own. People in love must have a desire to truly know each other. The word *love* has been overused and distorted, but perhaps, deep in our hearts, we know what love truly is. It's patient. Caring. Not proud. Tender. Serving. Gentle. Hopeful. Affirming. Life-giving. It builds up. Restores. Preserves life. It's pure. Beautiful. Fierce. Wild. Passionate. Sincere. Authentic. Sacrificial. It honours. Respects. Treats others with dignity. Protects. It's loyal. Faithful. Compassionate. Courageous...

"Instead of robotically programming mankind, our Creators gave us one rule back in the garden: not to eat from the tree of knowledge of good and evil. The fruit, if eaten, would allow mankind to determine for themselves what's good and evil. But God needs to determine that. And there was one creature in the garden who desired to be God himself. He tried to take over heaven. There was a huge battle, and a group of rebellious angles was thrown out of heaven, falling to the earth.

"Disguised as a serpent, our enemy got the first man and woman to question God's love and goodness for them. He suggested that maybe God was holding out on them, that life might be better if they ate from the tree. Convinced, they ate of the very tree that God had warned them not to eat from, warning them that they would surely die. And that's what happened! Their true identities as God's children died, and they took on the very nature of the enemy, who passed on to us the very opposite nature of the one we were created for. Now we feel guilt, shame, humiliation, darkness, fear, anxiety, rage, and hatred… all things that didn't originate from God's good heart as a Father. Our consciences were darkened so that we couldn't fathom God's light.

"Because of our new fallen nature, we hide from the very one who made us. God knew exactly where to find us and get us back. But so many of us choose to stay in the garden forever, living in eternal brokenness. God made us leave his presence. Before doing so, he created clothes to cover our shame and promised one day to not only cover but completely remove the darkness from us. Over the next thousands of years, mankind struggled to regain what we had lost: right standing with God, identity, wholeness, fulfilment, and purpose. We attempted to fill the God-sized void in us with everything and anything, participating in every kind of evil and darkness we could imagine. Yet underneath all that God saw something so precious to him. He would do whatever it took to get us back. So he spoke through his prophets of all mankind of a great light shining out in the darkness. The vision was for all the captives, the downtrodden, and those in spiritual darkness to be set free and washed clean on the inside.

"We forgot our maker. We didn't listen to his voice. We questioned his essence. So God put in place a system to make us ceremonially clean, using the blood of animals. But it wasn't enough to wash away the darkness and heal our seared consciences, which still remember what we were made for: an intimate relationship with God for all eternity. Unless a person's conscience becomes too seared, we are only able to go so far in wickedness. To help guide us, God set up 613 laws and ten commandments—if you break one, you break them all. This was meant to show us how far we had fallen short of who we are meant to be in perfect unity with him. Along with our desperate need for a Saviour, these laws point to Yeshua Christ, the Son of God who was to be born into the world.

"God knew from the beginning that the only way for us to be made right with him and reborn with our original identity and nature would be through a perfect sacrifice. He would have to sacrifice a being of his own flesh and blood, completely without fault or shadow. So his Son came to the earth as a man, knowing the Father perfectly. They were completely unified. As a man, Yeshua only said what he heard his Father saying, and spoke only what was on the Father's heart. He healed, set the oppressed free, and raised people from the dead from a place of right relationship with the Father, with the Holy Spirit at home within him. Yeshua came into the world to testify to the eternal truth of who God is and preach his word, which lasts for all eternity. God longs for intimate relationship with all mankind. He desires to be in their midst always, to love and be loved by them.

"The only way for us to be made right before God was for Yeshua to become the perfect sacrifice—meaning that he had to die in our place. Personally, it rings true for me that the Father never left Yeshua and was with him as he died. Neither did the Holy Spirit leave. But the enemy, with our help, wasn't able to destroy the Creator. We aren't more powerful than the one who made us. So three days after Yeshua died, he arose again. After his resurrection, he appeared to his disciples and many others in his new body.

"The Father, Yeshua, and the Holy Spirit did these things so that all our wrongs towards them and one another could be forgiven, removed and never again mentioned by God. Yeshua was whipped and bruised beyond recognition so we could be healed and recognized by the Father, to whom we had become unrecognizable. When we give our whole lives to Yeshua, because we believe in him, we are rescued and redeemed. We are re-created as the people we were always meant to be. When we give

Yeshua our whole lives, he gives us his life and right standing with the Father. This is the best news anyone could ever hear! Because we all deserve to go to hell and live in hell on earth. But God, by his grace and mercy, saved us from that fate. There is awe and wonder in this. God's mercy and grace are new every single morning. Only by faith in Yeshua can we be rescued from ourselves, from our distorted perspectives and mistakes, from the things we wished we'd never said, did, or thought. Believe that God through Yeshua Christ won the complete victory on the cross and by the power of his Spirit rose from the grave! By believing in Yeshua Christ and having confidence in him, we receive radical redemption and the unmerited favour of God."

This was a lot of information to take in, and both Ronald and Bella looked a bit overwhelmed by it all.

Tina smiled gently. "To help you understand all this, we'll share our stories with you. We want you to know how God has brought redemption into our lives. Every single day, we realize how weak we are, how in need of God we are. All good things come from him, the Father of lights. We all have the potential to imagine and attempt horrific acts, and we are not exempt from this. No one is. Humanity's fallen nature is capable of great evil, violence, and destruction. We can't control everything that happens to us. We can't control the ones we love. We can't control the world. We fall short and don't always love well. We make mistakes and then repeat those mistakes. Nevertheless, we are dearly loved and are part of an unshakable kingdom. We desire God's word to be at the centre of our lives. It's our purpose. We've decided to go after God—his heart, word, and kingdom—with everything we are. In the process, we have begun to be transformed from the inside out… something that is impossible in our own effort."

FOURTEEN

"My utmost desire is for my life to testify of the goodness of God," Trent said. "My life is a testimony of the power of God. May he be glorified through my life! I want to share with you the depths of his goodness, power, and love. But before I share, what does your heart cry out for? What are your longings?"

After a moment, Ronald raised his eyes to meet those of his listeners. "I long for my life to have purpose and meaning. I want to do something worthwhile and have a lasting legacy."

Bella thought about her own answer for a moment. "I want to be loved unconditionally as I am. I want people to see and know the real me, the woman inside, the one no one else seems to know. I don't want to be valued and esteemed because of what I do or how I appear."

"It's an honour and privilege to hear about your hearts' desires," replied Tina. "I want to live with purpose, intention, and passion. Something my heart longs for is an authentic community, one that's accepting without a hidden agenda and open to discussing things that others don't agree with. But I also long for the things you both shared. You aren't alone. I think those desires are written on the hearts of every person on the earth, even if they don't recognize it or know how to voice their deepest desires."

There were a few moments of quiet before Trent jumped back in to tell his story.

"When I was younger, I remember reading in Revelation that the elders continually cast their crowns down before God. I remember reading about the continual worship that takes place in heaven. I recall thinking, why? Is that all we would do? That's it? After we get to heaven, will we do nothing but cast our crowns before God? I wanted to know why. I can tell you that I now understand! I have gotten but a small taste of the goodness of the Lord, and now I understand."

He watched Bella and Ronald closely.

"Do you have questions? Maybe you feel confused? Do you wonder about what to do with your lives? Maybe you have questions about your sexuality? Your identity? Do you feel alone, like nobody understands you? That no one cares? Do either of you feel worthless or struggle with depression? Do you suffer from mental illness of any kind? Suicidal thoughts? Who has fear in their lives? Fear can take many forms. Does anyone struggle with addiction? Pornography? Alcohol? Do you look to other people for your worth? And when you don't receive it, are you left feeling as if you've done something wrong?"

In answer to Trent's questions, all four people put their hands up—including Trent.

"What?" Bella exclaimed. "I thought Christians had all the answers. Don't you have everything together?"

Trent shook his head. "The truth is that none of us are perfect, but God loves us anyway. At the same time, he doesn't want to leave us as we are… which my story will demonstrate. There was a time when I experienced all these issues for myself, yet I can tell you with complete confidence that the God of the universe, the one who made you, has come to set you free and redeem you! He has come to give you life, and life to the fullest! Even before he created the foundations of the earth, he loved you. He continues to love you and will never stop, no matter what you do. Your worth and identity isn't based on your actions. The one who created you knows you better than you know yourself. He loves you. Right now, he is calling you home, back into a relationship with him—and he has done it all. He has made the way. We've all fallen short and chosen our own way apart from him. We've all sinned! Frankly, I'm a great sinner… but then I met a greater Saviour: Yeshua Christ! God's Son was sent to take the punishment I deserved and bring me back into union with the God who created me. Yeshua took my shame and my guilt, freeing me."

Bella interjected with a burst of questions. "Trent, can you prove that the God you speak of is different than the one often portrayed in religion as angry, judgmental, or condoning of great evils? I'm thinking of evils like what happened at the residential schools here in Canada. What about historical genocides? I've also heard scripture used to condone the slavery of women and children. Some religious groups argue that women shouldn't be allowed to speak in public gatherings because of what the Bible says, or they say women have to wear very specific clothing."

Bella sounded bitter and angry as she shared her questions.

"My own story will show that what religion has taught us about God isn't really true, in a way," Trent said. "Religion takes a partial truth and twists it, removing the relationship we have with God and others. I thought God was angry and ready to strike me down if I ever made a mistake. Instead, I found a God who loved me so much that he sent his Son to die on the cross so I could be free and live in union with him. It's sin that God hates, though, and he is jealous for us. Sin separates us from him and he'll have to judge sin, because he is just and holy. But oh how he loves us.

"Listen, when I was a child my parents took me to a Catholic church. At the time, my parents didn't believe in God, but they went to church because their parents had gone to church. I'm not trying to bash Catholics. All I'm saying is that I experienced religion there. Religion says things like, 'Do this and God will accept you' or 'Confess to a priest and say three Hail Marys and your works will get you into heaven, so try to be good.' It's nothing but shame and guilt heaped onto you. So at the age of thirteen, I said to God, 'If this is what it's about, I want nothing to do with you.' I walked away and stopped attending church.

"You know, my mother always told me to be wise about who I hung around with. She wanted me to befriend people who would encourage me and, as she described it, keep me on the right track and going places. I didn't want to listen to her at the time, but I wish I did. She was right. My friends introduced me to pornography. A part of me knew it was wrong, but I got hooked. I fell into the cycle of sin—and let me tell you, it is a very slippery slope. I've seen things I wish I never had. I feel such regret, but I've also felt the grace and mercy of God.

"I also experienced bullying in middle school. It was constant. Although a lot of my friends would say these were amazing years, for me it was a dark time. It led me to depression and suicidal thoughts. I remember thinking one day how easy it would be to just step in front of a bus and end it all. I just wanted to be done with the pain. But I never shared what I went through, not with anyone. I thought I was alone. I understand now that I was never alone." He gave Bella and Ronald a hard look. "You are not alone! If you're struggling, tell someone!

"When I was seventeen, one of my friends invited me out to his church camp for a youth retreat. This friend was always in trouble, even with the police, but I noticed a sudden change in his life and didn't know what had caused it. So I went. It wouldn't have called myself an atheist, but you could say I was agnostic at the time. God was in my face all weekend. I fought it hard, and one night, while sitting around a campfire on a beautiful star-filled night, I got up and told everyone that there was no way for us to know whether God existed. The thing is, I didn't really mean it as a statement. I was crying out, 'God, if you're there, prove it.' The Bible says that if you ask God with a sincere heart, he will make himself known to you. Well, I wanted to know if he was real. I had to know! 'God, are you there? Show me! Is there more to this life than what I see, than what I've experienced?'

"I'll never forget what happened next. This precious memory brings great delight. The following evening, a storm blew through and took out all the power, forcing us to have a candlelight service. I remember holding my candle while we sang hymns. Suddenly, it was like my eyes had been opened for the first time in my life. Joy and love rushed in. In all my life, I had never experienced anything like it. No religion could ever do this. This was God. He was real! He had answered me… and he loved me! That night, I told the Lord, 'I'm in.'

"For the next few years, I attended a youth group and went to Bible studies. They were great, but I eventually fell back into old habits. Pornography, masturbation, fear, lying, and so much more. You didn't know me then, but I was very good liar. I could weave a story. It's not something I'm proud of. I fell into depression again as well. Some days I woke up with no hope. That's a terrible way to live. I've been there and I understand. There is hope, though, in Yeshua… the hope of glory! He loves us as we are and won't leave us. We are meant to be in relationship with him, with the one who made us. He came to set us free from the works of the devil.

"Despite this, instead of allowing God to take his place in my life, I turned to other things, even though all good things come from our heavenly Father. He is the one that satisfies! But I turned to people, movies, food, and pornography, trying to satisfy my needs. Nothing ever could. I was about thirty years old and weighed almost three hundred pounds. Both of my parents had passed away and my sister was living in Winnipeg. I had spent so many years lying to her that our relationship was almost non-existent. I also began to have trouble with my heart and this scared me.

"It had been years since I'd been to church and a friend of mine kept asking to take me. To get her to shut up, I finally agreed. I took her offer and went to church for the first time in quite a while. I will never forget what the pastor said: 'One day you are going to stand before God and you won't be able to hide anything. It will be as if you're naked.' When I heard these words, it was as if God was speaking right to me. I said, 'Lord, I don't want to come before you considering how I live right now.' But he loved me too much to leave me where I was. By his grace and mercy, I'm standing here today. He is worthy. He is holy. He is light. In him, there is no darkness! Well, I got on my knees and in tears repented for the way I had been living. I asked him to forgive me, and that's when I truly gave my life to Yeshua.

"After that, I got sick for about six months. In fact, I thought I was going to die. I thought I would never run, dance, or bike again. It was such a lonely and difficult time, but Yeshua was with me. My life turned around, almost in an instant. Things I had struggled with suddenly broke away. My eating habits changed and I began to lose weight. I lost a hundred pounds and began to run, dance, and bike. The word of God became real as the Holy Spirit gave me revelation. I was chosen before the foundation of the world? He had given me every spiritual blessing? He really loved me? Had adopted me?"

Trent beamed at the other three.

"I'm telling you right now that God loves you all so much more than you can imagine," he continued. "Just look at the cross! Come to him! Taste and see that the Lord is good! The Lord brought me joy and peace as I grew to love him more and more. Everything I thought I knew about him, everything religion had been trying to say about God, turned out to be twisted. The more you spend time with someone, the more you get to know them. Spend time with God in his word, in prayer, and in worship, and I'm telling you, you won't be disappointed. He loves you all so very much.

"In the relationship with my sister, God showed me that he wanted me to make things right. I had prayed for three months before I called her. And when I did, I told her how sorry I was. I told her that I had been wrong. That's it. God restored that relationship. Thank you, Yeshua! And guess what? He sent me to Ukraine to work with orphans! That's awesome, right? When I felt the calling, I told the Lord that I didn't want to work with kids. But then I said, 'If this is of you, I will go. Just make the way and I'll go.' Well, I didn't even have to lift a finger. My work happened to give me a bonus and my church raised the money for me in one morning. 'Okay, I'll go, Lord.' This turned out to be one of the most amazing experiences of my life. It impacted and changed me. I found my calling and passion. It's what he called me to do in my life, even before the foundation of the world! Isn't life great? Soon I was planning to go to Ukraine as a full-time missionary. I also started helping out with the same church camp where I had first experienced God.

"But be on guard for the devil, who goes around like a roaring lion! Around this time, I met someone who took my fancy. Well, listen to your closest friends and family when they talk about the person you're dating. Sometimes they can see things clearer than you can. This woman in my life had been married before and was separated, but she wasn't divorced. Do you see a problem already? I saw red flags but didn't take the warnings. A part of me still looked to people for my love and acceptance. Although this woman started out trying to honour God in our relationship, it took a very passionate and sexual turn. I would stay over at her place and she would stay over at mine."

As Trent was sharing, he grabbed his backpack and took out his Bible. He flipped open to a particular page, all the while continuing to talk.

"The relationship quickly became emotionally abusive. Two years in, I was but a shell of myself. My joy was gone. My self-esteem was at an all-time low. I had chosen my own path, and it wasn't the one God wanted for me. By the end of 2013, I knew I had to leave, but I had nothing left. I remember crying out to him and repenting. I told God how sorry I was. I had known this was wrong and needed his help to get out of it."

Trent paused for a moment, looked down at the page, and began to quote a passage of scripture.

> I love the Lord, because he has heard my voice and my pleas for mercy. Because he inclined his ear to me, therefore I will call on him as long as I live. The snares of death encompassed me; the pangs of Sheol laid hold

> on me; I suffered distress and anguish. Then I called on the name of the Lord: "O Lord, I pray, deliver my soul!"
>
> Gracious is the Lord, and righteous; our God is merciful. The Lord preserves the simple; when I was brought low, he saved me. Return, O my soul, to your rest; for the Lord has dealt bountifully with you.
>
> For you have delivered my soul from death, my eyes from tears, my feet from stumbling; I will walk before the Lord in the land of the living. (Psalm 116:1–9, ESV)

"God loves his children," Trent continued, lowering his Bible. "He loves you! And when you cry out to him, he answers. He's the God of second chances. Even third, fourth, fifth, and on and on. If we turn to him, he will heal us. Well, it still took me ten more months to have the strength to leave that relationship. But God… That's one of my favourite phrases, by the way. 'But God…'"

He took a moment to breathe deeply. His voice was full of passion, humility, and amazement.

"But God put me in a church that was so welcoming and loving. It was a place where his Holy Spirit moved and could begin to bring healing. He put a family around me so I could be myself and grow into the person I had been created to be. He places the lonely in families! And then he sent me to Costa Rica. Twice! Once as part of a missions trip with the church, and the second time was with Youth with a Mission to take part in one of their discipleship training schools. Another day, I'll tell you more about it. But on that trip, God showed me my identity as his son. He showed me that my acceptance, value, and love all come from him. He is the source. Everything I need is found in him. Everything.

"I had struggled with masturbation and pornography for a long time and knew it wasn't right. I knew that it separated me from God. I tried everything to rid myself of this sin. I wanted to be free of it. And then the Lord spoke to me and said, 'It is by my Spirit and power, not your own.' One night, I asked Yeshua to show me this sin on the cross. He did just that. The vision only lasted a split second, and it wrecked me. I cried out, 'Lord, forgive me. It's not by my strength, but by your Spirit!' Bam! He delivered me. By his Spirit! His power! His strength! And if Yeshua has set you free, you are free indeed! Yeshua loves you!"

FIFTEEN

The shadows had begun to grow long and it was getting to be dinnertime, so Trent offered to go downstairs to the cafeteria and get some food for everyone. He still had a couple of peanut butter and jam sandwiches, but there wasn't enough for all four of them.

"Does anyone want something other than water?" he asked.

Bella asked for an orange juice and Ronald requested a coffee.

"Surprise me," Tina said.

While Trent was gone, Tina began to share her own story.

"All my life, I considered myself a Christian, but I never truly grasped what it meant to be made right before God by faith in Yeshua, rather than by works. I didn't understand the reality of not living up to his standards. The God who created us is so perfect and holy that his standards are too high for us to fulfill. By breaking even one rule—by lying, for example—we are actually guilty of breaking them all. When we hold unforgiveness, feel jealous, compare ourselves to others, and secretly judge people, we are just as guilty before God as murderers, kidnappers, rapists, thieves, robbers, and those who are sexually immoral. That's how high God's standards work. We all fall short of his glory.

"Yeshua was fully God and fully man, in constant close relationship with his Father through fellowship with the Holy Spirit. He was able to live perfectly, even though he was tempted and tested in every way. While living on the earth, he was innocent, harbouring no guilt, fault, or moral shadow. By choosing to die for us, the ungodly and guilty alike, Yeshua paid the price for mankind failing to meet God's standards, which is death. Now all who believe can confidently trust in him and make him Lord in our lives. This permanently frees us from the problem of failing to meet God's standards. Through repentance, we are spiritually crucified with Yeshua. Our old nature, which failed to measure up, dies and we are raised to new life in Christ's resurrection and made new. We are completely clean, restored to our Creator, and fully free. A new beginning!"

Tears began to pool in Tina's bright green eyes.

"Just talking about it makes me feel overwhelmed," she said, her voice breaking with emotion. "God's grace, radical love, and mercy makes me undone! His words are truly life-giving! I love God with all my being because of what he has done through Yeshua for me to be his daughter. By his mercy, through the perfect sacrifice of his Son Yeshua, I am forever forgiven of breaking his standards! By grace, through my faith and living in perfect union with God's Holy Spirit, I can continue to live from his righteousness. His righteousness is only imparted by faith in Yeshua. It cannot be earned. It's a priceless gift we must all choose to accept. Or we can choose to refuse it. Every day, even moment by moment, I face the choice to put my trust in God, to surrender my life afresh and allow him to lead me. I must admit that I don't always get it right. I'm in a process of maturing, stretching, and growing as Yeshua's life is made fully manifest in my life.

"It's one thing to hear stories of what God has done, but it's another thing to encounter his love and presence for yourself. He's here right now, longing for you to come home in his unconditional love. God originally made mankind for himself, to be his sons and daughters. By faith, we are made anew into the sons and daughters we were originally intended to be."

The door opened and Trent walked back into the room, carrying drinks, sandwiches, and fruit. He promptly handed out the food.

The interlude allowed Bella and Ronald a moment to take in Tina's story. The way she'd spoken had been so raw and refreshingly authentic. It rattled something deep inside Ronald, making him felt uncomfortable. Memories flashed back of all the pain he'd caused and lives he'd taken.

In that second, Ronald lost control. It felt as if multiple attackers piled on top of him, pressing him with a very heavy weight. His face reddened in anger and his eyes glazed over, filled with extreme hatred.

As the others watched, his body thrashed uncontrollably. His lips curled in a snarl and his hands went up in a boxing stance.

Bella jumped to her feet and backed up to the wall behind her. Trent and Tina also got up, flanking him on either side, one on each side of the bed.

"Stop," Trent commanded with authority. "Be still, demons, in Yeshua's name."

Immediately Ronald stopped moving and completely stiffened up.

Tina leaned in close. "Ronald, can you hear me?" The question was met with silence. "Open your ears and loosen your tongue. Ronald, can you hear me?"

Faintly, and with much effort, Ronald whispered, "Yes, I can hear you."

"Do you want to be completely free?"

"Yes, I do."

"Right now, confess and repent to God of every evil thing you've done," Tina said. "Ask Yeshua, who is here, to set you free. He will do it gladly because he loves you. What sins do you need to confess and repent before God?"

Slowly and gradually, Ronald began to speak. He picked up speed as he went. "I confess and repent to God for murdering innocents and criminals... for hating him, myself, and my fellows... for sleeping with multiple women and drinking to dull my pain... for stealing, lying, and cheering on others in wickedness... for selfishness, judgment, gossiping, and giving in to rage... for bitterness, unforgiveness, hatred, and self-hatred..."

Trent put his hand on Ronald's back and commanded him. "Get out! In Yeshua's name, *get out.*"

Loud shrieking noises came out of Ronald's mouth, and then his whole body went as loose as a ragdoll. Ronald blinked, once again feeling completely like himself with a clear mind.

"Ronald, you need to give your whole life to Yeshua," Tina said. "Otherwise the demons that just left will be back, and they'll bring reinforcements. You'll be much worse off than before. Do you want to surrender everything, your whole life, to Yeshua?"

Straight away, Ronald responded. "Yeshua, as much as I've messed up, you have set me free! I give you my life, though I don't know why you'd want it."

As a small child, Ronald's old man had been a sergeant in the army, forcing them to move often. In the secret places of the house the boy had found blueprints, guns, black outfits, and gloves, among other discoveries. There'd been so many layers of deception that Ronald hadn't ever known who his dad really was. They were never close. As a drill sergeant, he'd demanded that Ronald be self-sufficient, beating him into submission and keeping the house spotless.

Every week or two, his old man had brought home boxes of liquor, pizza, and new violent movies. If Ronald was quiet, he could join his dad in the living room. It was their father-son bonding time, at least until Ronald left to join the Navy SEALs at age eighteen. By that time, he'd hardened so much that he never showed even a trace of emotion, no matter what was happening or who was involved.

Men in army gear had regularly come over for poker nights. They'd set up the table, pull the blinds, and blast loud music. After playing a couple of rounds, they'd pull open the secret compartments in the hinged mahogany bookcases, taking out only what was needed. Those items could be hidden quickly should anyone come to the door—treasures, guns, weapons, maps, and even spy gear.

But the men were always careful never to speak of this in front of young Ronald. Even so, he often heard his father's friends confiding in one another. And sometimes they bought the boy's silence with bribery, using money and small gemstones. Other times, when the men were competing against each other or trying to get the best of his dad, they would bribe Ronald for information about his dad's activities in college. And sometimes they even sent young Ronald on errands with secret messages.

The truth was that he had been raised to be a spy, to compartmentalize information and keep secrets. Later in life, he kept many secret hiding places in his room. There was a thick Latin book on his shelf which had been hollowed out to hide the proceeds of all these bribes. At the right time, he planned to use it to start an assassination service, once he had established some trustworthy networks.

Everything changed when Ronald turned five. One night, his dad went out with his army buddies for a job that went bad. After an explosion at a weapons facility, Ronald's old man was the only person to survive. He was sent to the hospital with third degree burns, and of course this raised many questions. However, there was no proof. And with his army training, he couldn't be easily swayed into telling anyone what had really happened.

After Ronald's dad was discharged, he started to drink more heavily, and consistently, to deal with the guilt and pain of what had happened that night. Easily enraged, he took it out on Ronald and his mom.

A few days before Ronald's eighth birthday, he stole the cookies his mom made—and then? Well, life had been proving more than she could handle, so she left Ronald behind with his angry father. Neither of them heard from her again. It was as if she dropped off the face of the earth.

That year, his birthday fell on a Saturday. He spent it hiding in the forest from his drunk father, pretending he was a highly trained assassin and a hero. Ronald vowed never to let anyone hurt him again. He would keep everyone at arm's length, fight back, and find ways to get even. He had so much pain, anger, and darkness inside. So he embraced it and allowed the darkness to drive him. He dreamt of being the best assassin in existence and making every person who'd ever hurt him pay with their lives.

Later that year, Ronald found a secret shack deep in the forest, a forgotten reminder of the outlaws and slaves who used to travel at night through the area. He turned the place into a hideout and never told anyone of its existence. This is where he hid the treasures, maps, plans, and spy gear taken from his father's hiding places. His father's guns were placed in a metal box, although Ronald was smart enough not to use them until he was properly trained. They were untraceable, and one had been designed to be taken apart so it could be transported in secret.

With everything squared away, he put a new padlock on the door and always carried the key on a necklace.

When he was eleven or twelve, Ronald found a punching bag, gloves, and a fighting instruction book at school. He snuck in at night, dressed in black and covering his face and hands to keep himself from being identified. He broke a window and disarmed the security alarm, just like his dad would have done.

Back at the hideout, he set up the punching bag and began to teach himself to fight and defend himself. Through his teenage years, he learned self-discipline in order to control and direct the burning anger inside.

Ronald chose to stay in school and earn excellent grades to keep up the charade that nothing was wrong, that he was an ordinary young man. A loner, yes, but smart, strong, and determined. He put in hours of weightlifting at the school's gym. He also picked up odd jobs around the city, using the money to feed himself.

At the age of eighteen, after completing high school, the first thing he did was sign up for the SEAL training. It was a gruelling process and only the best of the best passed. They had to be willing to have each other's backs. It was a matter of trust in life-and-death situations.

Ronald kept his focus on the dream of being an assassin, developing his cover so no one would suspect his true motives. All the while, however, he felt a gnawing emptiness deep inside.

He ignored it, refusing to let the pain control him. He avoided any sort of emotional attachment.

Discipline and determination got Ronald through his SEAL training. He adapted, as required, to look out for the others, not just himself. But he still didn't allow anyone to get close. He became an expert at reading people and remained watchful for those who might one day serve as contacts for high-paid assassination work. Patience was critical, as was compartmentalizing information.

After training was complete, Ronald and his class were given a reprieve. He crashed for two days, then went out and found a lady of the night to celebrate. She made him feel like a man. They went to an expensive restaurant and afterward rented a cheap motel for the night. When Ronald left in the morning, he caught a glimpse of the pain in her eyes. He ignored it and brushed aside his feelings of guilt. He had to remain invincible; no one and nothing could stop him.

Once in a SEAL team squadron, Ronald met Connie for the first time. When he remarked that women weren't cut out for combat, she put him flat on his back before he even realized what had happened. After a dazed moment on the ground, she gave him a hand up and commanded that he never insult another woman like that—or else.

Immediately, Ronald respected her. And Connie never held that one-time comment against him. For some strange reason, she always looked for the best in people, even in the worst of humanity. Somehow she knew exactly what, when, and how to say anything that needed to be said. She once told Ronald that she saw him as a man who lived by a code of honour, integrity, and discipline. He lived with determination and a strong sense of purpose. He was someone who could shoot for and hit anything he wanted by going after it, not holding anything back.

Something about Connie was starkly different compared to everyone else on the team, but he didn't understand what. She was confident without being arrogant, decisive with a good head on her shoulders. She wasn't one to stand for bullying, cussing, or gossiping. She sought to do her best, protect her teammates, and get the mission done.

A deep part of Ronald desired to look out for Connie, to be there for her at the drop of a hat and live the best life he could. Being around her made him put his secret dreams on the backburner. In the meantime, he patiently added to his skills, knowledge, and resources. He still took thorough mental notes on when, where, and how to acquire black market technology, but the dream was left to simmer, as though it were a pot of stew.

Truth be told, these months with Connie were the best of his life. Even with the gruelling tests and active combat, he felt alive. Still, he continued to numb the pain, and recently he'd been feeling weighed down by the memories of what he'd done to others. Voices shouted in his mind and heart, telling him he'd never be able to live any differently. The memories played on repeat, forcing him to relive the most regretful moments of his life. It seemed impossible to change, so he drank until he could briefly forget the memories.

No one besides Connie had ever seemed to care about Ronald. They'd never expressed any interest in hearing his story. They were too focused on fulfilling their own needs. Connie had cared, and slowly he had opened up her. But she never pushed him to share anything he wasn't comfortable with, respecting his privacy.

Connie seemed lighter, happier, and more hopeful than the others in their unit. Ronald could see no reason for it. They saw people in terrible circumstances. Whole cities and towns were bombed. They killed people for a living and saw the darkest sides of humanity. Child soldiers. Sex trafficking. The murder of whole families. Suicide. Genocide. Rape. It was a never-ending parade of death and darkness.

One day, after pondering it for some time, Ronald finally asked the question: "Connie, why are you so different than the rest of us?"

She responded quickly: "Yeshua!"

"Shut up with that hogwash—"

"I'm serious, Ronald. Yeshua is the one who makes me different!"

"How can a dead lunatic make you different?" Ronald asked, truly beginning to wonder whether he was falling in love with a crazy person.

She just smiled at him warmly. "Ronald, I know and believe with all my heart that God loves me. Why? Because Yeshua, who was completely innocent, hung guilty on a tree for me. He died so I can be made right with the God who made me!"

"You're crazy, Connie."

With that, Ronald walked away.

From that day on, he called her Crazy Connie. To which she would reply, "I'm Crazily Loved Connie! Worth dying for! Loved beyond measure!" She'd go on and on about how much God loved her and had died for the whole world.

Every time, the preaching went over Ronald's head. In one ear and out the other. Sometimes he would blank out and have no memory of anything Connie had said even though she'd been talking for twenty minutes.

But then came that fateful day when Connie took a bullet for him. She died when it should have been him… and it cracked Ronald to the core.

He never admitted it to anyone. Nor could he explain what happened.

Instead he tried focusing again on his dream to become an assassin. As he perfected his natural talents, he became like a Tin Man with no heart. He developed new techniques to evade security. And he wouldn't just kill with guns anymore; he would use more unconventional methods, including poison, arson, suffocation...

When he was fully immersed in the life of an assassin, executing people for payment and at the top of his game, he felt nothing inside. He was empty, and nothing could fill that emptiness, not even women and the money constantly rolling in. He went on twelve or more assignments in a single month, and he had the time, patience, and mental capacity to handle the work.

But then something broke, just like when Connie had died for him.

One day, a seven-year-old girl ate the poisoned candy that had been meant for her mother. That girl's death gave Ronald a nervous breakdown and he couldn't return to the field afterward—that was, unless he wanted to get caught. He had lost something.

At the advice of a secret mentor, he decided it would be best to take an early retirement. He cut all ties with his contacts, liquefied his assets, and moved to a new city. He bought a low-end apartment, believing he deserved no better, and began frequenting the bars every night just to numb the pain long enough to see another day. He couldn't imagine anyone would want him. The voices in his head taunted him endlessly.

For the next thirteen gruelling years, Ronald lived to drink, barely getting by and sometimes waking up with no idea of where he was or how he'd gotten there. He would go home and crash for twelve hours only to get up again, eat something, and go out drinking again.

Eventually Tin Man Ronald got to the point where he'd had enough. He would end it all.

And that's when something happened he would never have expected. He encountered Love personified and truly came home for the first time.

SIXTEEN

When Ronald decided to give his life to Yeshua, Bella freaked out and didn't know what to think. She needed time to process everything.

Tina suggested they all go for breakfast the next day to give Bella the time she needed to make a decision. She also gave Bella her phone number so they could make arrangements to meet up again.

Once Bella had left the hospital room, Tina and Trent turned back to Ronald, who had a huge grin on his face.

"You should consider getting baptized," Trent suggested.

Ronald's grin faded for a moment. "What's baptism?"

"It marks the end of your old life and beginning of your new life in Yeshua Christ," Tina said. "Once you're baptized, you'll know God as your perfect Father, both in this life and the next."

As it happened, the hospital had a pool they used for physiotherapy. Trent called down and asked if they could use the facility as soon as possible. Although there were classes scheduled that same evening, and therapy sessions scheduled the next day, it turned out there would be an opening at 6:00 a.m.

Ronald planned to get up at 5:30, to give himself enough time to prepare.

Just before six o'clock the following morning, Trent came by with a pair of floral print swimming trunks and a bright blue T-shirt. He also carried his daily coffee and a new leather Amplified Bible.

Once Ronald had changed, the newfound brothers in Christ sat together reading God's word and asking the Holy Spirit to teach them. Trent turned to Psalm 116, explaining that it perfectly described what the Lord had done for both of them:

> I love the Lord, because He hears [and continues to hear] My voice and my supplications (my pleas, my cries, my specific needs). Because He has inclined His ear to me, therefore I will call on Him as long as I live. The cords and sorrows of death encompassed me, and the terrors of Sheol came upon me; I found distress and sorrow. Then I called on the name of the Lord: "O Lord, please save my life!" Gracious is the Lord, and [consistently] righteous; yes, our God is compassionate. The Lord protects the simple (childlike); I was brought low [humbled and discouraged], and He saved me. Return to your rest, O my soul, for the Lord has dealt bountifully with you. For You have rescued my life from death, my eyes from tears, and my feet from stumbling and falling. I will walk [in submissive wonder] before the Lord in the land of the living. I believed [and

clung to my God] when I said, "I am greatly afflicted." I said in my alarm, "All men are liars." What will I give to the Lord [in return] for all His benefits toward me? [How can I repay Him for His precious blessings?] I will lift up the cup of salvation and call on the name of the Lord. I will pay my vows to the Lord, yes, in the presence of all His people. Precious [and of great consequence] in the sight of the Lord is the death of His godly ones [so He watches over them]. O Lord, truly I am Your servant; I am Your servant, the son of Your handmaid; You have unfastened my chains. I will offer to You the sacrifice of thanksgiving, and will call on the name of the Lord. I will pay my vows to the Lord, yes, in the presence of all His people, in the courts of the Lord's house (temple)— in the midst of you, O Jerusalem. Praise the Lord! (Hallelujah!) (Psalm 116:1–19, AMP)

Shortly before they were about to go downstairs, the doctor came in to try and stop them.

"Ronald, you're still not well enough to be submerged," he insisted.

Before the doctor could get too worked up, Trent intervened. "What about if you come down with us and watch?"

In his heart, Trent asked Father Light to surprise the man and radiate his supernatural, redeeming love over the baptism.

On the elevator ride, Trent began to hear whispers from the enemy, telling him that he was unworthy, an outcast, and the last person who should ever be doing something like this. What were people going to think?

In response, Trent burst out in praise: "You, oh God, are my Father, and I am your son! I belong solely to you. All I am, all I have, is yours. Everywhere I go, I live for you alone, God, for the old me is dead and gone! He was buried in the grave with my King, Yeshua!"

The doctor looked at Trent in shock.

"Are you out of your mind?" the doctor demanded, beginning to get angry. "What the hell are you thinking? Stop that—right now."

Trent just continued. "You can't stop this, man. I'm so free from me that I'm free from you! I am so completely free! And I ain't going back to that old life of mine! Yeshua is my King and Lord. I live and breathe for him alone! He made me and set me free to live for him! Hallelujah!"

As the doctor went into a rage, screaming and calling him names, Trent realized that his old self would have apologized and shrunk back. But not this new Trent. He wasn't going to compromise the truth for anybody, under any circumstance.

"It's like I said, dude, I'm so free of me that I'm free of you," Trent replied. "I'm out of my mind and out of yours. Yeshua lives inside me. He wants to change the world. And in fact he just told me that you're angry at him because your mom and dad died in a car accident when you were young. My parents died when I was young, too. I was angry and a mess for a lot of years, man! But God kept chasing after me, showing me who I really am as his son. He healed me, set me free, and gave me a new heart and a new mind. Now I live for him. He's given me a reason and a purpose to live—and I can't give that up! I can't go back to my old life and deny all that Yeshua has ever done for me."

After this, the doctor went dead quiet. He just stared at the elevator doors, as though by staring he could make them open faster.

Trent nudged Ronald, silently prompting him to share what meeting Yeshua face to face had done for him. But Ronald had gotten uncomfortable by this point and remained quiet.

Ding!

When the elevator doors slid open, the doctor stormed out. He walked away, forgetting about his duty to ensure that Ronald was safe going into the pool.

"You're going to have to really learn to let go of everything and not live for yourself anymore," Trent said as they stepped out of the elevator. "Otherwise you're going to live by your feelings and allow life to shape you. You won't last long as a Christian that way. That's not the life Yeshua died for you to have. His word says that if anyone is to follow him, they are to pick up their cross, deny themselves, and follow him. It's called complete surrender. We've been called to give the Lord God our King our entire lives."

When they got to the pool, they found Tina in a bathing suit, already waiting for them.

"God, help me walk this thing out," Ronald said as he stood at the edge of the water. "Holy Spirit, I need you to teach me. Give me more boldness for you and your kingdom! Have your way with me and help me walk this out with you, in a perfect love relationship, with clean hands and a pure heart. Oh God, you are so amazing! I'm so grateful that your grace and mercy woke me up today, that I have one more chance to manifest you and represent you on this earth, empowered by your Holy Spirit! May it be done not by my will, Father, but yours! You are the reason I draw breath. Without you, I'd be dead. I love you more than life! You are my everything. My everything, Lord! All good things come from you, the Father of lights!"

Ronald looked up and saw the glowing looks on his new friends' faces. Tina in particular had the look of someone who was madly in love—and madly loved.

"Our God is so wonderful, isn't he?" Tina said as they approached her. "Are you ready, Ronald? You're at the point of your old self dying, so you can live for our Lord and Saviour, Yeshua Christ! There's no turning back now. We know that our lives aren't meant to be the same after we've been divinely impacted by God's power and love! Today is the day of the grace and glory of God!"

Ronald felt a hint of the importance of what he was about to do. He felt called upon to surrender everything to God—a God he couldn't see but whom he had now personally experienced.

"I am ready to die... whatever that means," Ronald said.

Tina smiled brightly. "Very good! Now put your towels by the wall and come with me into the water, gentlemen."

Trent and Ronald did so and then followed Tina into the water, jumping straight into the deep end of the pool. Just as they surfaced, Tina splashed them both! Ronald was taken aback—but not Trent, who immediately splashed back, launching a three-way water fight.

What happened next made no sense to Ronald. A dark-haired Indigenous woman suddenly ran out of the women's locker room and jumped into the pool. She swam over to Trent and jumped onto his back.

Mid-splash, Ronald stopped in astonishment. The lot of them were laughing hysterically for some reason. Together, Tina and the newcomer were trying to dunk Trent's head underwater. Half-succeeding, Ronald dived downward, swam to Trent, pulled his legs out from under him, and then let go! The result was that all three went underwater and came up conceding the match.

"You win, Ronald," Trent exclaimed once he'd caught his breath. "But watch out for some friendly retaliation! By the way, this is my fiancée, Mandy!"

Ronald nodded to the woman.

Together they waded to the shallower end of the pool, where they could stand with their feet firmly planted on the bottom of the pool.

"Let's continue this joyous occasion by confirming why we're here," Trent said. "We're going to baptize Ronald as he publicly devotes his life to our Creator God. Ronald, please come and stand in front of me."

Ronald moved in front of him and crossed his arms over his chest, as Tina demonstrated. Then Trent put one hand behind his friend's head and gripped him tight.

"Ronald, do you freely and fully surrender your life to Yeshua Christ, letting him wash you clean and make you into a new creation? Do you die to your old self, your old life? Do you publicly declare that Yeshua is your Lord and Saviour?"

"Yes," Ronald affirmed. "I want to give him my whole life."

"Take a breath and relax." With that, Trent turned Ronald and dunked him to his right into the water. "I baptize you in the name of the Father, Son, and Spirit."

Once fully immersed, Ronald had a sense of perfect love washing him clean from the inside out. But in the midst of this sensation, something deep inside screamed.

"No!"

He recognized the voice. It was the version of him whose life had revolved completely around himself. He felt a life-and-death struggle for control between the old man and new man. As this battle raged, the Holy Spirit suddenly arrived and empowered Ronald's spirit to overcome his flesh. Given a spiritual dagger, he drove it into the heart of his old self.

Trent lifted him out of the water.

"Rise," he declared. "Rise in his resurrection, recreated as if man never ate from the forbidden tree. Reconciled to God, the Creator of all things."

Coming up out of the water, Ronald realized that he'd never felt so alive. Full of passion, he felt excited for to undertake this new life with God. Joy overflowed in his heart and he knew without a doubt that God loved him, even though he who had done so much wrong. God had chosen him, and that meant the world to Ronald. God considered him worth dying for!

In some way, it was as if Ronald saw the world clearly for the first time, with a heart full of love, compassion, grace, and mercy. He was a whole new man, by faith in Yeshua Christ, having been baptized into his death and resurrection.

As he drew a deep breath, he made the commitment to never again live as he had before.

SEVENTEEN

After Ronald's baptism, Tina felt a prompting from the Holy Spirit to check her phone, which she had put on silent since arriving at the hospital. She congratulated Ronald, officially welcoming him home into the kingdom of heaven, and headed out of the pool.

"What's up, Tina?" Trent asked.

"The Holy Spirit is prompting me to check my phone. We'll see."

Tina dried her hands with a towel and then picked up the phone. She blinked upon seeing the twenty-one text messages and fives missed phone calls, all from Bella.

"Something is going on with Bella," Tina said. "She's repeatedly asking me to call her back."

She hit the redial button and put the phone to her ear.

Bella answered after the first ring, sounding very excited "Tina! I met Yeshua last night! He is real and loves me beyond measure!"

Tina was so excited that she took the phone away from her ear, held it out at arm's length, and shouted, "Yes! Thank you, Yeshua! You are so very good, Papa! Thank you for bringing your daughter home. You've won!"

She burst forth with joy, jumping up and down. She spun in a circle.

"Everyone, listen up!" she called. "Bella met Yeshua last night in a dream!"

Tina took a breath and then put the phone back to her ear.

"Welcome home to the family, Bella. I'm so excited for you. Come on over to the hospital pool so we can baptize you right away. Just bring a change of clothes. Then we're all going out for a celebratory breakfast."

"All right," replied Bella. "I'll be there in about fifteen minutes!"

As soon as Tina hung up, Trent looked at her teasingly. "I think the whole hospital could hear you, Tina! Hallelujah! Yes, Yeshua!"

When Bella arrived, she put down her bag and ran over to the pool's edge! She immediately dove into the deep end and swam over to where the others were playing in the water and praising Yeshua.

When she came up, Tina gave her a great big hug. "Bella, do you want to be baptized into the life of Yeshua? In the name of God the Father, Son, and Spirit?"

"Yes, I do," she responded emphatically.

"Then I baptize you into Yeshua! Hold your breath and rest your arms on your chest."

Bella did as she was instructed, and then Tina dunked her backwards into the water. Upon being lifted back out, Bella felt refreshed deep inside where she'd previously been dry and weary.

Tina felt hot, like she was on fire from the inside out. Trent, too, felt the fire of the Holy Spirit all over his head and hands. As for Ronald and Mandy, they felt full of exuberant joy and a zest for life. Everyone felt excited to be alive, made right through Yeshua, completely accepted in a way that no human being on earth could ever take away.

In the midst of this tangible moment, everyone was simultaneously touched by the Holy Spirit, who had just come to dwell in both Ronald and Bella.

"Let's take this party out of the pool," Trent suggested as he began to help everyone out of the water.

Even as they exited, they felt the Holy Spirit's presence increase, raining down even more of his fire, restoring and empowering this passionate group of friends. Everyone stumbled to the change rooms as if they were drunk. Drinking of God's perfect love was better than drinking the finest wine of this world!

It took a while for everyone to get ready to go out for that celebratory breakfast. They all seemed to just want to sit and get lost in the love they had been made to live in.

By the time Trent and Tina were ready to go, they noticed an older woman sitting in a wheelchair by the pool, dressed for swimming. As Trent looked at her, he felt in his heart God's tender love as a Father.

As they walked over, Tina felt a surge of pain in her hips and back.

"Good day, ma'am," Tina said, bending down in front of the woman. "Are your back and hips hurting?"

The woman replied sharply. "They hurt like hell after being taken apart and put back together nine times! All because the stupid doctor didn't do the surgery right fifteen years ago! Why the hell do you care?"

"God is letting me feel your pain right now," Tina explained. "That means he wants to heal you! Can my friend and I please pray for you?"

"I don't believe in all that crap. He ain't ever done nothing for me."

Trent listened intently to Holy Spirit, who was communicating his Father's heart for this woman, even in her hurt, anger, and obvious brokenness.

"Do you want to be healed, ma'am?" Trent asked.

"More than anything," she replied. "But it's impossible. The doctors say it can't be done, and I don't believe that any higher power…"

Tina gave her a compassionate smile. "You don't have to believe. Just allow us to pray for you."

"Fine! Do it and then leave me *alone*."

Tina placed her own hand reassuringly on the woman's hand. "Be healed in Yeshua's name!"

The woman suddenly stiffened. "What did you do!? My back feels like it's on fire!"

"Yeshua loves you," Trent said. "He's showing you his love by healing your back. Can you try standing up?"

Flabbergasted, the woman began to shakily stand.

Heal her hips, God, Trent prayed.

Immediately the Holy Spirit spread the fire that had started in her hips. Tina stood up and stepped back as the woman stood before them, strong and free. She took a few steps, then a few more, and then she began to run! In fact, she ran all the way to the deep end of the pool and jumped into the water. As Trent and Tina watched, the woman swam all the way to the end, got out, grabbed a towel from the bench, and then ran back into the women's change room.

She never came back, but that was okay. Yeshua was pursuing her and wooing her heart to her heavenly Father. He would make sure this seed got watered and began to grow.

Soon the group was gathering again in the front foyer of Tina's apartment building. As soon as Tina got there in her SUV, she led them upstairs to her third-floor unit.

Trent smirked as he detected the delicious smell of breakfast already wafting out from inside the apartment. "Tina, did you call Ethan?"

Tina looked at them innocently. "Who, me? No, I wouldn't do that!"

"Yes you would," Trent said. He turned to their new friends. "Ethan is a fellow friend in Christ. He's a chef, and he carries the presence of peace everywhere he goes, the peace Yeshua gives that passes all human understanding. Ethan is a humble man with strong, confident faith in Yeshua and the power of God through the cross. Come on inside and we'll introduce you!"

Inside, everyone took their shoes off at the door and entered the short hallway to the kitchen. A man of medium height stood at the stove making pancakes. Past the island counter was a set table with bowls of strawberries, whipped cream, bananas, syrup, and chocolate chips.

Tina practically tackled Ethan with a hug, which made everyone laugh.

"Ethan! You are truly an amazing brother in Christ," she said. "I'm so thankful for you, and proud of the man of God you are!"

Ethan turned in Tina's arms to wrap his own arms around her. "And you, dear, are also amazing! A dear treasure to me who is worth protecting, who enriches the lives of those around you."

"This is brother Ethan," Tina said by way of introduction to the newcomers to their group. "Ethan, meet Ronald and Bella. Come on in and make yourselves at home!"

Tina offered everyone hot drinks, which she assembled and distributed with the help of Ethan and Trent. Each one was served in a china teacup. There was also a pitcher of water on the table with a glass at each setting.

Once everyone was seated, Tina asked Trent to thank God for the food. He then broke out into a rap.

"Yo, Lord! We thank ya for this food, this radical time in yer faithfulness. To ye belong all the passions and delights we have! We all owe ya our very lives. Thank ya that we all are blessed to be a blessing. In Yeshua's name, amen!"

Ethan grabbed the hot pancakes and began to pass them around, starting with Ronald on his left.

"Geez, man, it's like you are Mr. Perfect," Ronald commented to Ethan. "The chicks must really dig that."

The others, except Bella, all burst out laughing.

"Well, actually, Ronald, I'm still in a process of changing and growing," Ethan said. "I still make mistakes—and when I do, I repent to the Lord and apologize to those around me. But by completely trusting in Yeshua and the word of God, those mistakes are becoming less frequent. This happens as I pursue a lifestyle of righteousness, holiness, and passion for God."

Bella turned to Ethan. "What's your story? How did you end up being so on fire for God?"

He grinned and a twinkle came to his eyes. "It would be my pleasure and honour to share what the goodness of God has done in my life!"

As he spoke, Trent stood up and got the covered tray of crepes from inside the stove. He brought them to the table and began to pass them around the table.

As everyone took the crepes and added toppings of their choice, Ethan shared his story.

"God has mightily blessed me," he began. "Because of his amazing goodness and abundant grace, I was born into a passionate Christian family. I believe this is the main reason I have been transferred from darkness to light, from one kingdom into another, completely free, washed clean, and made innocent in God's eyes. He's done this for my whole family since my father found Yeshua when he was twenty years old. We served God full-heartedly, loving and honouring him in private as well as in public. As a result, we valued and loved everyone we knew without condition."

There was a pause as everyone ate, taking this in.

"You have a strong family legacy, Ethan," Tina remarked. "You have strong values and a strong foundation based on faith in the truth of God's word. You've been established as a son of God in complete confidence and trust in him. Please continue!"

Ethan took a bite of his crepe and swallowed it. He didn't seem bothered at all by the fact that everyone else was chewing. He knew that his testimony was building faith in all those who heard it, that every word brought glory, praise, and honour to God.

"As a child of about five, I remember asking Yeshua for the first time to come into my heart," he continued. "My father led me in a prayer of trust in Yeshua as Saviour, saving me from darkness, sin, and a self-focused life. I believe that this specific moment was my most important, despite being very young. The passionate love and faith of my family gave me confidence to approach God's throne of grace and mercy. I could trust in him as a child because of the pure examples of those around me. Ever since, I've been walking with Yeshua. Yes, I've had my ups and downs, my own issues and shortcomings, but by the grace of God I've remained pure, devoted, and dedicated to him as a young man. Whereas many go into the world or taste the worldly life, I've cultivated a hunger for more of God and his word, fixing my gaze on him and trusting what Yeshua has done for me by dying and rising again.

"Although I was raised in a Christian family involved in ministry—and yes, I've been greatly influenced by that—I made the personal decision and commitment to follow Yeshua. It comes down to making daily decisions to trust in the wondrous love and leading of God. I take him at his word that he will lead his children through the storms of life. During my years as a youth, I went up front many times at revival meetings to give my life to him. I also remember one evening in high school when I lay everything down in front of God—and I mean everything! You name it, I gave it to Yeshua: my future, my wife, my work, my finances, and everything else! I saw his pure goodness and knew him to be worthy of everything I am. Every good thing in me and in this life comes from God, so I keep giving it all back. All these beautiful happenings can be counted as strong and wonderful opportunities to give my life to Yeshua and follow him. Yet that one time when I asked Yeshua to come into my heart as a child was a special salvation moment. In my heart, I know that I've been saved ever since childhood."

Now it was Ronald's turn to interject. "Wait a minute, man. What the heck do you mean by being saved?"

"Saved? I would say it means that I've put my faith in Yeshua. I've received his work of salvation in my life and believed that his blood has cleansed me from all sin. I've made Yeshua the Lord of my life. He is the only way to the Father and everlasting life. I'm saved from condemnation and hell, which never was the plan of God for me or anyone else. I am now God's beloved son, loved and fully accepted by him. I experience a Father-son relationship, Yeshua has become my friend and King, and the Holy Spirit lives inside me. God is with me and will never leave me. I get to experience his companionship and relationship. I have found my true purpose and identity in Christ as his loved son."

Bella spoke up, too. "Ronald and I were baptized in water today, and after I came up the presence of a holy being filled me. It became hard to move, yet I was filled with such awe, wonder, and reverence for God. What's your story, Ethan? Did you get baptized in water and filled with this same holy being?"

"In 2008, I was baptized in water," Ethan said, nodding. "After that, I made a commitment to live out my personal faith. About a year before, I received the baptism of the Holy Spirit, who is the holy being you sensed today, Bella. For me, this resulted in the speaking of tongues, which is a heavenly prayer language. Sometimes when we pray in tongues over a person, the Holy Spirit will allow us to hear exactly what's on the Father's heart for us."

The Holy Spirit stirred Tina's heart to elaborate more on what Ethan had shared.

"We must all seek to be established in God's love and identity as a daughter or son," she said. "The truth is that we are all a new creation by faith in Yeshua Christ alone, not by works. It's by faith in his finished work that we're changed from the inside out and transferred from the kingdom of darkness into the kingdom of light. The Father delights in all of his children and longs to hold those who are hurting in his arms. The Holy Spirit, whom he breathed into us, is described as a jealous lover who intensely longs for more and more of us. Yet his love is so pure that he forces himself on no one, giving us the choice of whether to accept his love. God keeps offering it to people, even after they've refused to accept this gracious gift.

"Let us all grasp this even more clearly. Perfect love casts out all fear. Not some, or a little, but *all*. Yeshua died for us so we might be made right before the Father, in whose sight we'd be innocent, righteous, and flawless. When we refuse to put our trust in Yeshua as the only way to the Father, we stand before God condemned and guilty. There is no other way. In our best efforts, we can never get it all right. Our heart's loyalties can stray and we can be deeply affected by the brokenness everywhere we look. That's why living before the Lord's face is our saving grace, for the troubles we face can feel exhausting. But God...!"

She went on to quote a passage of scripture she had read that very morning:

> For you know that your lives were ransomed once and for all from the empty and futile way of life handed down from generation to generation. It was not a ransom payment of silver and gold, which eventually parishes, but the precious blood of Christ—who like a spotless, unblemished lamb was sacrificed for us. (1 Peter 1:18–19, TPT)

Next Tina began declaring a poem of phrase to God.

> My heart is most satisfied when I trust in the Lord my God,
>
> In whose depths I am revived and come alive.
>
> I want to know Yeshua so that I may become like him.
>
> He died for me to be restored back to God,
>
> Throwing my past into the sea of forgetfulness.

Knowing him because I consider my past to be garbage,

I fix my heart and devotion on the one who died and rose again.

By grace, through faith in Yeshua, I am whole and set completely free.

My life is a love song for the Maker of heaven and earth.

I trust completely in God alone.

He alone is worthy of all glory, honour, and praise.

Yet in his grace, he bestows gifts of his grace upon

Those who call on Yeshua's name.

My heart is overwhelmed at the goodness of our God!

The very fibres of my being were made for the love of our Creator!

I was created uniquely as his wondrous masterpiece!

Our Creator God wants to know and be known by each one of us!

In his presence, fear cannot stay.

There is room for only one Master in my life!

Today, and everyday, we choose to whom

We will give everything, for my choice is to trust the Lord Yeshua,

Who gave his life to set me free!

Nothing is impossible for the one who sets my feet upon a firm foundation!

Christ is the solid rock on which I stand!

He brings me out into a spacious place
where I am secure and safe.

He trains my hands for war and readies
my mind for battle.

I set my focus on the Lord, who gave it all
for me to be

Made right before him, completely free of
fear,

Living in his confident trust as a

Devoted and passionate lover of the King
of kings.

I am honoured and privileged to be united with Yeshua by faith.

He died believing that it would be enough
to make all right before him.

When we are in dark times, we trust that
the Lord will see us through,

Working all things for our good and for
his glory.

After she finished her poem, he found that everyone around the table was giving her their full attention.

"Every day we are tested in our faith, and some tests are bigger than others," Tina continued. "Living in the Spirit, as God calls us to do, isn't easy, and sometimes we're asked to go against everything we've ever known. There are times when God asks us to leave our comfort zones because he's more interested in the condition of our hearts than in our comfort. He also asks us as his children to give up our old ways of doing things and walk like Yeshua on this earth. As we walk with God, we learn from the Holy Spirit how to love a lost and dying world."

With this, Tina suddenly turned to Ethan.

"Ethan, may I ask you a question?"

He nodded.

"What is one major test of faith you've faced?" she asked.

Ethan gave this some thought. "One of them was a relationship that didn't work out. This was very difficult for a long time, and a long journey, but through it God taught me to trust in him! And I ended up being fully healed and restored in my heart from the sadness and depression. God is faithful! This was a testimony of his faithfulness to bring healing and carry me through any difficulty."

Mandy chimed in next. "I'm so amazed and thankful for the goodness of God, otherwise I'd be dead right now!"

"What do you mean, Mandy?" Ethan asked. "How have you encountered the love of God?"

"I knew nothing about God or Yeshua," she admitted. "I'd heard really bad stories about people getting hurt by religious groups. Some even died. Others lost loved ones. I wanted nothing to do with that and saw no good thing in the stories I heard. Then one day I got really sick and could hardly move without help. My parents were living their own lives and seemed oblivious to my existence. Yet my sister came and stayed with me. It was a hard and humbling time, because I had to ask for help.

"One night I felt so empty, so weighed down and helpless, that I couldn't help but wonder what the heck was the point of this thing we call life. Then I heard a voice say to me, 'If you don't admit everything you've done wrong and give your life to me, you'll die tonight without knowing the love you were made for.' I realized that I didn't want to die without ever really living. So I asked, 'Who are you, Lord?' And he replied, 'My name is Yeshua of Nazareth, and I died, then rose again for you. I'd do it again if you were the only one of my children to return home to the Father!' Well, I poured out my heart and soul, telling him every single thing I'd done wrong and all the secret hurt in my heart. Baring my soul and feeling completely exposed, I heard him tenderly whisper, 'I love you, Mandy. You are mine.' After that, I gradually started to get better.

"On a trip to a thrift store, I saw a Bible among the other books. I had no idea where to start reading, but Yeshua led me to start in John. I was eager to hear more about the one who had revealed himself to me in the dark night of my soul. Trusting in him turned on a light inside me and gave me a reason to get up in the morning. I sought to get to know the one who gave his life for me."

"Wow, Mandy!" Tina exclaimed. "That's powerful! We're blessed to hear your testimony, for testimonies build in us the faith to ask God to do these things again." Her smile was so wide. "How about the rest of you? What helps you build trust in God and walk out your faith on a daily basis?"

Ethan cleared his throat before answering. "For me, I value the growth of my relationship with God and my intimacy with the Holy Spirit. I spend time every day meditating and reading the Bible. Worship, prayer, and praying in tongues are basic, perhaps, but they play a vital role in filling me up, refreshing me, and renewing my mind. I also aim to live my life with a clean conscience, walking in purity and holiness and repenting of my sins whenever needed. Although I realize I still have some growth to do in my identity as a child of God, I greatly value my true identity: I am deeply loved by my Father in heaven as his child. I choose to accept and receive his boundless love for me. I am highly valued and accepted by my Father, despite my sinfulness. I live through his wonderful grace and love. I am saved not through deeds but through faith in Yeshua Christ. This is something I hope others can see in my daily life. I've also noticed that hunger is one of the keys in my life. Hunger for more of him, to see his supernatural power manifest and his kingdom advance on the earth. If I lose this hunger in my walkabout with him, I could easily drift away from the Lord.

"The Bible also speaks of our responsibility to maintain a clean conscience, speak the truth, cling to what is good, and hate what is evil. We are called to honour God and others even when they don't deserve it, or when we have been hurt by them. Because honour is part of who we are. When we come together, we can share stories of God's goodness and faithfulness. Peace and love flow even in times where we're still or quiet with other believers. There is strength in numbers and we all need one another. We are stronger together. We each are strong and weak in different areas, having experienced God in different ways. We are responsible for what we choose to believe, but thankfully we can ask the Lord for help and the Holy Spirit will reveal truth so that lies won't have any place in our lives."

Mandy was nodding along as Ethan spoke.

"Childlike awe and wonder," Mandy said. "They also help to build faith. I'm personally amazed to hear of people who in the hardest of circumstances still trusted that God was *way bigger* than their problems. They kept seeing beauty in the pain they were in."

All of a sudden, Tina's phone buzzed. It meant someone was at the front door and wanted to come up to see her. When she answered the phone, she immediately recognized her sister's voice on the other end of the line.

Yeshua, I need your help, she prayed. *My sister needs your all-encompassing love.*

"Hi Ashley," she said. "I have some friends over for a spontaneous breakfast, but you're welcome to join us!"

After hanging up, Tina turned back to the table.

"My sister Ashley is coming up," she added.

A swell of the Father's compassionate love for Ashley arose within Tina. She and Trent shared an understanding look across the table as they waited.

The source of Ashley's bitterness and hurt had begun when she and Tina were kids. She had always been quieter, more shy and soft-spoken than her outgoing older sister. At home, it had been difficult to find her voice. On the playground, she was bullied and befriended by girls whose home lives were far less than ideal. Ashley's gift of empathy often led her to invite them to share their burdens, yet she often felt like a dumping ground for al the junk these girls carried. That made her feel unloved and less than everyone else.

When she was a teenager, Ashley had trouble fitting in at school. She couldn't find anyone who wanted to be her friend, except for Brent. This jock on the football team noticed her and sensed her venerability. Figuring her for an easy mark, and not truly caring about her, Brent befriended Ashley in Grade Eleven after Tina had already graduated and moved out west for college.

Ashley's loneliness and lack of other friendships had made her vulnerable to Brent's charming advances. At first he had made her feel special, loved, and pursued. Gradually he convinced her idolize his perspective over that of everyone else. He began to isolate her from her family.

During the summer before her senior year, she gave herself to him fully and they had sex under the tree at the lake by his parents cabin.

Immediately Ashley regretted what she'd done and tried to hide her shame. She wore the guise of still being a "good girl."

And though concerned and loving, her parents didn't know how to reach her.

Things took a turn in the fall when Ashley discovered she was pregnant and told Brent. He demanded that she get rid of the baby. The thought broke her heart.

That night, she told her mom, dad, and older sister everything. Together they forged the difficult road ahead. Ashley finished up her senior year with a modified schedule and gave birth on Valentine's Day the following year to a girl named Jane. Her aging parents helped their youngest daughter as she began life as a single mom.

Brent practically ignored her, treating her like a piece of garbage.

When Jane was five, the girl suddenly took sick and died when her grandparents were out of town. Between her breakup with Brent, the regret over what she'd done, the loss of her baby girl, and accumulation of pain over the years became too much to bear. Ashley became bitter and blamed everything on those around her.

Ten years later, Ashley's walls were high, fortified with the brick and mortar of deep pain. She kept them at a distance, not allowing her heart to love or be loved by anyone. She sought nothing but survival and had no vision for her future.

Now thirty-three years old, she walked around with a dark gloomy cloud overhead, drifting in and out of relationships with men who didn't know how to treasure her heart. All they did was use her for their own needs, only to dump her after.

EIGHTEEN

When Ashley walked into the apartment, it seemed as if the whole atmosphere changed. Her demeanour was very dark, but Tina went over and greeted her sister with a hug.

"I'm glad to see you, Ashley!"

"How much longer are they going to be here?" Ashley asked in a whisper. "You know I don't do well with strangers or crowds."

Tina's response was gentle and soft, spoken in a low voice for only her sister to hear. "I don't know, dear Ashley, but you don't need to be afraid of them. You're in a safe place. These new friends have just stepped into a journey of discovering who they truly are. Come in and I'll introduce you to everyone."

Ashley took off her shoes and put down her purse. The sisters walked over to the table where everyone remained seated. Tina introduced Ashley to Ronald, Bella, Trent, Mandy, and Ethan.

Mandy was sensitive to the Spirit and change in the air, sensing that the sisters needed time alone together.

"Bella, I want to bless you by buying you a new Bible and journal," Mandy suggested. "Can you come with me? We can go shopping, and then you could drop me off at my place."

Bella nodded. "Sure. I need to get ready for a shift at the hospital anyway. As I said earlier, it sounds worthwhile to get into the Bible for myself and ask the Holy Spirit to teach me the truth. I want to know for myself how my Creator sees me and learn to hear his voice."

Both Mandy and Bella got up to leave, but Trent also spoke up.

"Ronald, do you have a place to stay right now?" Trent asked. "Do you need help with anything?"

"Yeah, I've got a small apartment, but it's a pigsty. I'm going to need help cleaning it. Not to mention cleaning my inner life up, man. Could you help?"

Trent smiled with enthusiasm. "Sure I can, bro! Let's get you a new Bible and pick up some cleaning supplies along the way… and anything else you need. You can even stay the night at my place."

As everyone got up, they thanked Ethan for breakfast. Everyone's mouths overflowed with blessings and gratitude as they said their goodbyes.

Ethan quietly began to clear the extra dishes from the table. "Do you ladies want anything else to drink?"

"I could go for a cup of chai," Tina replied.

Ashley doubted Ethan's sincerity and trustworthiness. "No thank you."

"Alrighty then," Ethan said. "Would you like me to heat up a couple of crepes for you, Ashley?"

A sudden stomach growl betrayed her hunger. "Sure," she mumbled.

Ethan grinned. "Okay."

He picked up the crepe dish and took it into the kitchen, where he found another plate and loaded it with three more crepes. As he reheated them, he filled the electric kettle. Then he went about the process of gathering dishes from the table and putting them in the sink. As he bustled around, he kept praying in the Spirit for the sisters.

Ashley sat down and was soon eating breakfast, loading her plate with the leftover toppings.

"Isn't there someplace else you'd rather be right now, Ethan?" Ashley suddenly said in a burst of bitterness. "Why are you serving two women and doing women's work?"

Refusing to get into an argument, he just kept washing dishes. "Nope. There's no place I'd rather be."

"Well, I don't trust your act. Men are only out for one thing... and they only look out for number one. No, I don't trust the whole lot of you. For far too long, your kind has dominated our society, brutalizing everyone in your care—"

"Ashley!" Tina interjected. "I know you're hurting, but that doesn't make it right to lash out at him. You're my sister and I love you dearly, but Ethan is a brother in the Lord. I can't stand to see you acting like that. I know this isn't who you truly are!"

Ashley rolled her eyes. "You're still buying into all that trash we were spoon-fed from the cradle? Not one person ever showed me that they were any different after 'surrendering' their lives to God. They just kept right along doing what everyone else did—talking, acting, and living the same way... pretending they're perfect, like they have everything, standing in judgment of everyone else, deeming others as less than, selfish, horrible, messed up, not worth the time of day... worthless! Oh, the trash I hear from so-called Christians on Sundays while working as a waitress. No, there is no God. If there was, every single person who claims to be Christian would live differently. But there's just as much greed, lust, anger, gossip, lying, rage, fear, insecurity, and toxicity inside the church as there is outside of it. Religion makes me sick! Why bother trying to please some invisible being who sets up standards that are impossible to meet?"

By the time she got to the end of her diatribe, she was practically shouting.

Tina could feel her sister's pain deep in her heart. Her own tears threatened to spill as Tina thought about the full extent of Ashley's painful story. There were some parallels between what had happened to Ashley and to Tina herself, but now was not the time to point that out. For now, Ashley needed to know that she'd never been alone in her suffering.

In heaven's throne room, Father Light watched the scene unfold, glad that Ashley was being so honest and frank about where she was at. He wanted to get her to the point, though, where she would willingly give him every shred of her pain— and in return, accept his healing love. He deemed Ashley as worthy of love.

"Why would such a loving God allow such brokenness in the world?" Ashley continued. "I hate feeling so empty, broken, and worthless. For so long, I felt like it was expected of me to have everything together. To be there for people, to live up to their expectations. And all the while, my own life was a dumping ground. Where is the protection, help, strength, new life, healing, transformation, and provision God has promised in his word? Why doesn't it seem like God listens to me? Why is he so far and distant? So I came to the conclusion that he must not exist. Or at least, everything isn't as he claims it to be. My life is so empty and futile. What's the point of even existing when all I feel is pain and emptiness? My friends always seem to want something from me. I don't feel safe with anyone. I have to do everything on my own. People tell me how nice and sweet I am, but what about the days when I don't feel that way? I often feel much darker. Depressed, anxious, overwhelmed, fearful, sad... upset. Would people really want to be my friend if they saw how ugly and messed up I get? If I lose courage and get triggered by fear at the smallest comment? If I lust after non-existent dream relationships that have no basis in reality? If I struggle to know what to say and feel at a loss for words? If I feel judgmental? If I feel annoyed when someone asks for my help? Why does it seem like I always have to be what other people want me to be? Why is there so much pressure to look, act, behave, or think a certain way? Back when I believed in God, why did I give everything only to fall short? I'd get upset with people just because I didn't get my own way. I always felt the weight of pressure to represent Yeshua well to those who didn't know him. But Yeshua gets everything right all the time. How can I compete with that? I can't emulate him. I really can't! I feel like what God asks of us is impossible. So I walked away from everything. I found comfort and love, however limited or conditional, in the arms of a woman. Then another and another. I also find comfort and a sense of control in the food I eat. For a short time, I'm okay, but then the overwhelming emptiness returns and I feel weighed down, depressed, anxious, and guilty again."

As Ashley shared, Tina's heart broke for her sister. But Tina knew that Yeshua was present in dark times. Only God's love, and the price Yeshua had pain with his blood, could heal Ashley's brokenness. God never intended for his children to live in brokenness! He created humans to be loved in relationship with the Holy Trio.

"Ashley, you asked me why I still believe," Tina said. "The truth is that I didn't believe for most of my life. I tried to do everything right all the time, but I failed miserably. I withdrew from everyone who loved me and viewed myself as unworthy of love. In that place, Yeshua saw me in my mess and said, 'I want that one. I'm willing to do whatever it takes to make her my own.' He is in the process of perfecting me. I'm only right inside when I live from a place of surrender to him, when my eyes are securely fixed on Yeshua. Without him, I think I'd have ended my life long ago."

As this sank in, Tina burst into another poem:

> As a child, I was frightened of shadows, of doing anything wrong.
> The world was terrifying and I sought to get by, only living to survive.
> I found refuge and safety by withdrawing into isolation,
> Expressing to none the pain my heart was in,
> Desperately looking to be understood and loved as I am.
> I even doubted that my parents loved me,
> Believing everyone was against me, no one on my side,
> Shoving closed the door to my heart.
> Yet my emotions were evident to many on my face,
> For a broken spirit makes the face look bleak.
> My heart's ability for emotional attachment and love seemed limited.

Joyful, fulfilling life and pure passion
seemed impossible.

But there is a love so pure and powerful
that it can change anyone and everyone.

It is offered to everyone, free of charge.

Experiencing this love full force causes
one to give up everything

To the one who expressed pure love by dying in our place,

Having committed no treachery.

He died as a rebellious traitor or murderer.

I wrap my heart in faith of the one who
died in my place,

He who took all my fear, shame, hurt,
guilt, darkness, and all I've done wrong

Into his body, nailed to a tree, taking the
punishment I deserved,

Leaving it there so I can live completely
free

In the perfect love I was made for!

You are my fire, oh Creator God,

The lover of my soul!

I seek to be wholly devoted to you

Every single day.

As Ashley sat in the chair at the head of the table, Ethan
came over and knelt before her.

"Ashley, the Father is showing me his heart for you personally," Ethan said. "I see a picture of you as a princess at the
centre of a fierce battle. Two kingdoms are fighting aggressively
for your heart and affections. One seeks your ultimate destruction and the other seeks your healing and complete freedom.

Which one will you choose to rule your heart? Through his grace, God gives us faith. He knows exactly what our hearts need to hear, see, or feel for us to believe in him. He's so creative that he constantly creates new opportunities for his children to experience the Father's love. God wants to embrace you in your brokenness, to wrap you in his all-encompassing love and heal your shattered heart so you can experience his goodness for yourself and choose to trust him. At times, you've been hurt by men, misunderstood and abused when you should have been protected. At times, they haven't loved you. Maybe they've taken advantage of you. Maybe they stopped you from thriving in the gifts, passion, and calling God has given you. For all this, whether it was intentional or not, I ask for forgiveness on our behalf. I also bless you in Yeshua's name, praying that you may discover the wonder of his love and grace."

As Ethan spoke, Ashley began to shut down. The door to her heart was swinging closed. The food in front of her was forgotten, she looked towards her sister.

"I'm sorry, Tina. I need to go. I can't stay. I'm so sorry for what's about to happen."

The sisters stood up and embraced one another. Tina's heart was breaking in love while Ashley's was shattered. It seemed as if her heart was inaccessible.

Tina squeezed her sister and spoke tenderly. "Call me if you need help. Day or night, I'm willing to be there for you. I love you, Ashley, so very much! You are a priceless treasure hidden in darkness. Neither God nor I will ever give up on you! Your life has value, purpose, and meaning. You are loved and accepted as you are."

Without responding, Ashley left the apartment. Tina didn't want her to leave, but she also knew that she couldn't force her sister to stay.

Perhaps God does the same thing with us, she thought to herself. *He allows us to leave so we might realize how much we need him.*

Tina turned to Ethan. "Can you please pray with me for my sister? This isn't the life Yeshua died and chose her for. The battle is fierce right now—for her very life, I think."

Ethan agreed, and together they appealed before their Father in the courts of heaven, praying in the Spirit for the deliverance of their sister Ashley.

At that moment, Father Light was walking on a beach with one of his precious sons. He also listened to the cries and desires of Tina and Ethan as they interceded for Ashley.

Large waves lapped against the beach as Father Light walked barefoot in the sand next to a young boy, Timmy. The beach was surrounded by grass, trees, flowers, and open meadows. A river ran down from distant mountains into the ocean of love.

This was one of Timmy's favourite places to come with Father Light.

"Help me understand," said Timmy. "Why did Yeshua choose to die?"

"My son, Yeshua chose to die because he believed all mankind was worth it," explained Father Light. "We decided to stop at nothing to bring our children home again, once they'd been lost, even if it meant risking everything for the chance to get you all back. When my children live in a place of complete trust and surrender to me, it's easier for them to hear and recognize my voice. I'm always wanting to speak with my dear children. Are you hearing and listening…?"

Ashley stepped outside of her sister's apartment building and felt like the sunshine was an insult to the storm of emotions inside her.

"Why me, God?" she whispered. "Why has all this bad stuff happened?"

She felt like she was at the end of her rope and couldn't handle being around people anymore. Suddenly she remembered a secret place by the park where she and Tina had used to play as kids. She had considered visiting that spot before but hadn't ever followed through. There was a tree there which they had climbed. They'd played tag and hide and seek for hours around it. She also remembered them bringing their journals and staring up into the clouds—dreaming, listening, and asking questions. Trusting that God was good had seemed like second nature.

As the years had gone by, she'd found the pain and brokenness around her too overwhelming. When questions came to her, they went unanswered. Fear and despair were a heavy burden on her heart and there seemed to be no evidence of changed lives in the people she knew; they appeared to be no different than those who didn't believe in God. Wars continued to rage, divorce tore families apart, cancer and tragedy claimed lives far too young, and evil ran rampant, apparently unchecked, all over the world. Children died of starvation! Orphans were homeless, forced to sell their bodies for scraps of bread! God looked to be so far away.

Ashley remembered her father, who'd hardly spent any time with his daughters. He had been too busy. He'd felt like a stranger at times. He was always doing something, or at least planning to do something. His fierce schedule appeared to be his master. How could she ask him her burning questions when he struggled so much himself?

To Ashley, following God had always looked like following a long list of rules. On the other hand, the most passionate people she knew in the real world were those in the LGBT community. At least they desired to help people, to change the world and feel confident in themselves. In contrast, she so often heard Christians speak ill of others, complaining, judging, and criticizing. They were so fearful and insecure! She heard whispers of those who used porn, abused drugs, and slept around outside of marriage. What room was there in the church for a woman like her? She didn't see any way to do things differently than the way they'd always been done.

She was tired of always being told what to do, or what not to do, so at the age of fifteen she had walked away from her faith. The lack of goodness in the world troubled her. Why didn't Christians bring about more positive change? She imagined that she and God were at an impasse, acknowledging one another's existence without caring about each other.

In the ten years since, Ashley had struggled to find her way and carve out a life for herself. During the day, she worked hard and was disciplined, like her father. In the evenings and on weekends, she partied. After being burned by men, she began to date women and found them to be more caring, even though they seemed to come with more emotional baggage. These relationships lasted far longer than with men, but ultimately they always ended. Nothing seemed to last. Only a few days ago, her latest girlfriend, Sandy, had texted her to say "We're done." No explanation. She hadn't even cared enough to say it to her face.

The weight of pain Ashley felt seemed overwhelming. She was losing her will to go on.

Suddenly, a little girl walked up to her with one hand behind her back. She had green eyes, olive-toned skin, and long, braided hair. She wore jean shorts and a T-shirt that said *Daddy's Princess*.

"Hi, pretty lady!" the girl innocently said. "No need to be sad, 'cause Yeshua loves you! All of you. He can see deep into the depths of your sea!"

With that, the girl began to walk away.

Before she got too far, though, she stopped and turned around. "Oh! The Holy Spirit just asked me to tell you that God doesn't promise a pain-free life. But he does promise to be with us no matter what happens. He's never left you, not even for an instant, and he's waiting intently for your return home!"

The girl ran up to hug Ashley's legs.

"Bye, pretty lady! God loves you!"

And then she ran down the sidewalk where a couple was waiting patiently for her. Together, the family walked off, hand in hand.

That's when Ashley heard a still voice she hadn't paid attention to for a long time.

"Ashley, I'm still here. I never left you. You were never meant to do this alone. Life is always better when done together in authentic community. My arms are open and waiting for you. Put your faith back in Yeshua, and you'll experience life like never before. I want you to truly know me in close relationship, but I'll allow you to determine what our relationship looks like. Faith and trust in me involves risk. If you want, go ask your sister, or maybe Ethan. You can either stay in the darkness and continue to pout, or you can put your trust in me and allow me to lead you out. The choice is yours."

Ashley thought more about her sister. Tina did seem to have a spark in her eyes, a spring in her step. Laughter and joy oozed out of her. Yes, something deep and delightful was being forged in her sister.

Just like that, Ashley recognized a longing within her heart for more, although she didn't know exactly what. Just hearing that voice from her childhood sparked hope in the darkness of her soul.

"I esteem my children by what's in their hearts, not their appearance," the voice said. *"That's one reason I give people the choice whether to be restored in relationship with me. I don't want slaves. I want friends, devoted lovers, and children who know who I really am."*

Still on the beach, Father Light continued speaking with Timmy.

"It's important that my children don't have a know-it-all attitude," he said. "Instead they should be humble and open, willing for me to correct them in love. They should desire to learn from me and truly know me as I am."

They walked a little longer in silence.

"When you're with other people, your perspective can be based on an illusion, or even a lie," Father Light explained. "This influences how you engage with each other. Truth doesn't flow freely. Words kill rather than bring life. Or they hang uselessly in the air because they serve no lasting purpose for my kingdom. And there are unseen creatures who attempt to get people to believe lies. But when my Son Yeshua sets you free, you are completely free. Not partially, but fully! However, it's imperative that you recognize that not everything benefits and builds you up. Your life tells a story every day to the world around you. Will you tell a story worthy of the price I've paid for you, Timothy? Will you dare to believe that I want to do so much more in and through your life?"

NINETEEN

U pstairs in the apartment, Tina and Ethan were continuing to pray for Ashley, with no knowledge of what was happening outside the building.

"God, I ask that Ashley would really know you as you are, that she would personally experience your tender love and heart for her," Tina prayed. "Let her discover the fullness of life that comes when we know you personally, daily walking with you living inside us, united as one with Yeshua, and with every step trusting that we are completely accepted and loved by you, Lord God."

The Holy Spirit gave Ethan a verse to declare in praise:

> God, you're such a safe and powerful place to find refuge! You're a proven help in time of trouble—more than enough and always available whenever I need You. So we will never fear even if every structure of support were to crumble away. We will not fear even when the earth quakes and shakes, moving mountains and casting them into the sea. For the raging

roar of stormy winds and crashing waves cannot erode our faith in you. (Psalm 46:1–3,
TPT)

As Ashley reconsidered her relationship with God, she
turned and began to walk back into the apartment.

"God, we place our trust in you, knowing that you are good,"
Tina continued. "My heart's in turmoil, aching for my sister to
know you, Papa, to experience and know your love and power
in new ways. But I know that walking with you in faith and
confident trust is a choice only we can make for ourselves.
Please show Ashley how much you love her, unconditionally.
Show her that you will never give up fighting for her. I remember when you revealed your faithfulness to me, always offering
the gift of new life you died for me to have. I said, 'No, I'm not
worthy of that.' But you were so devoted in love to me, even
when I was against myself. You never gave up on me. You kept
offering that gift, allowing me to choose whether to receive it
and follow you. When I finally accepted your lavish love for me,
God, everything changed."

Ashley stood in the open doorway of her sister's apartment,
shocked and in awe at the prayer she had just overheard. Tina's
faith was so confident, sure, and strong! It was built on a strong
foundation. Ashley heard that passion and wanted it for herself.

Just then, Ethan looked up, as if he'd been tapped on the
shoulder. "Ashley? Are you okay?"

Hearing his words, Tina looked up and noticed her sister standing at the entrance.

"I want what you guys have," Ashley whispered. "But I don't know how to get it."

In the blink of an eye, Tina jumped up and ran over to hug her sister. "Simply decide to trust that what Yeshua did to make us right with God. That's enough. Give him your life and allow him to change you from the inside-out. Define your identity by knowing your Creator. Make the choice to trust him, one step at a time, and you'll discover that he never left you!"

Ashley leaned back a step, to give herself a better look at her sister. "God just told me the same thing while I was standing outside the building."

"That's because he loves you right where you're at," Tina assured her. "His heart for you really is good and you can trust him with everything. He doesn't force himself on anyone, but his Spirit yearns jealously for more and more of who we are."

"Really? I didn't think anyone could ever love me that much."

"God isn't like anyone else. He's perfect, pure, and holy. He keeps his word, even when men can be proven to be liars. God's heart as a Father is so beautiful. When we see a glimpse of who he really is, awe and wonder stirs in our hearts. It's his desire that none should be lost, but that all would come to salvation."

Ashley looked sceptical. "What does that mean, Tina? Frankly, I don't know anymore, even though we grew up together in church."

"We can stand in front of God with no fear, shame, or condemnation, having free access to come before him anytime. We are welcomed home, Ashley, remade as we were meant to be—holy, chosen, and seen as a flawless child of God. It's not just about getting into heaven one day. It's about heaven making its home inside of us."

"Can we sit down?" Ashley asked. "This is a lot to take in."

"Yes of course!"

Tina led her sister into the living room where they sank down onto the couch. Ethan was already sitting there.

"What is the hope that you two carry?" Ashley asked as she got comfortable. "There's something obviously different about your lives, even though so much of the world around us seems meaningless."

Ethan responded first. "The hope we have is that all life has purpose, meaning, and value. It comes out of our personal relationship with our Creator God. We know that our lives have an impact. There's no one exactly like you, Ashley, in terms of your personality, gifts, and talents. No one can take your place. The contribution you can make has enormous value."

"No one can fully understand the struggles and pain of the human heart," Tina added. "But because God is like no other, he loves like no other. He's patient, merciful, compassionate, truthful, accepting, and inviting. He's so creative that he made everything out of nothing. He loves us so much that he chose to come and live as one of us, to live in this painful and broken world, even dying for us. As a leader, he served by washing those people who trusted in him, dying for the wrongs done by them... by all of us."

"People were made to love and be loved in relationship, just like birds were made to fly," Ethan said. "In getting to know someone, you spend time with them and ask questions. The answers reveal who a person really is, including what they value and stand for. We seek to listen to understand where they're coming from. Humbly lay aside what you think about them so you can truly know who they are. This all applies to our relationship with Father Light, Yeshua, and the Holy Spirit."

At this point, Ethan paused. He felt prompted to ask Ashley an important question.

"Ashley, what have you allowed to define you? Who are you?"

"I'm a woman who has known deep pain, betrayal, and loss," she replied. "I've looked to other people to define who I am and show me what life is about. Then they've abandoned me. I work hard and play hard. I've had jobs where I've felt undervalued and underpaid. I'm a free spirit who feels weighed down—at the end of my rope, as the saying goes, looking for a reason to keep going."

Ethan nodded to himself. "So basically you've allowed your relationships with people to define you. And when they haven't worked out, you've let the pain define who you are as a victim. Am I right?"

"Yes. I'd say that's accurate."

"Can you see any negative consequences from defining yourself based on your relationships, Ashley?" Tina asked.

Ashley paused for a moment or two to consider this question she hadn't been asked before.

"By basing my identity on relationships with others, I became very unstable," she said. "People's opinions of me change daily. And they turn out not to be committed to me in the long haul. Basing my identity on this pain has been very poisonous to my mind, heart, and maybe even my body. I've been moody, fearful, insecure, distrustful, and uncertain. I've wanted consistency and hated change. People sometimes seem to be resentful or judgmental of me, including because of my choice to be in relationships with other women. Maybe that's a negative consequence, too, of how I've defined myself. My heart has grown bitter, cold, and resentful. It's as if there's this deep, open wound in me that I carry around all the time. I'm like a giant nerve that gets triggered by even small comments. The pain of life sometimes feels like too much. I've thought of attempting suicide. I feel very hopeless, but I'm searching for a reason to hope."

Ethan nodded. "The reason I asked you this is to get you thinking. The Bible says that God allows us to follow our selfish desires when we choose to believe lies rather than the truth he speaks, and that following these desires has consequences. However, when we get to know our Creator and allow him to define who we are in the context of relationship, our whole lives change."

"Earlier you mentioned that you feel hopeless, but that you're searching for a reason to hope," Tina said. "What else is your heart longing for?"

"I long for unconditional love and acceptance as I am. To be esteemed and valued for more than what I do or look like. I long for something more in life, for purpose and meaning that lasts. For authentic relationships and connections with people who genuinely care about the real me. For boldness and courage to be who I really am, once I've figured out who that is."

Tina reached over to a side table and grabbed a purple Bible. She opened it to a particular book and chapter.

"During a season of change, of stepping out of my own comfort zone in faith because I believed God was inviting me into something new, the Holy Spirit highlighted a passage for me. Let me quote it."

> Keep trusting in the Lord and do what is right
> in his eyes. Fix your heart on the promises of
> God, and you will dwell in the land, feasting
> on his faithfulness. Find your delight and true

pleasure in Yahweh, and he will give you what you desire the most. Give God the right to direct your life, and as you trust him along the way, you'll find he pulled it off perfectly! He will appear as your righteousness, as sure as the dawning of a new day. He will manifest as your justice, as sure and strong as the noonday sun. Quiet your heart in his presence and wait patiently for Yahweh. And don't think for a moment that the wicked, in their prosperity, are better off than you. (Psalm 37:3–7, TPT)

"I share this with you, Ashley, to make knowing God the upmost focus and desire of your life," Tina continued. "I know he hasn't always been first in my life, but I'm hoping that you will join with me in this pursuit of knowing God as he truly is."

After their conversation, Tina gave her sister a copy of the movie *The Shack* for her to watch at home.

"I hope this movie will help your heart understand what a relationship with God is meant to look like and why so many bad things happen in the world," Tina said. "It should reveal the answer to the question of where God is when these bad things happen to us."

Ashley took the movie home, grabbed a soda from the fridge, and made a bowl of popcorn before sitting down in her favourite chair to watch the movie.

As the movie began, Ashley wondered about what kind of movie her sister had given her. On the screen, a boy named Mack was rushing home to protect his mom. He then got a beating from his father. Then a neighbour woman saw the boy with a bruise on his face and invited him in for a piece of pie. Her advice to the boy was to talk to God, who always listens.

Ha, Ashley thought. *I don't believe it. Where was he when I needed him?*

Ashley shouted angrily as the movie continued. The boy grew up and got married. Although the couple believed in God, Mack's wife's faith was deep while his remained shallow.

At the end of summer one year, he took his three kids on a camping trip. There, they met another family and roasted marshmallows together with them. At the end of the night, Mack tucked the kids into bed under the stars.

Everything seemed like a normal family outing, Ashley thought.

The next day, the two oldest kids went canoeing on the lake. After the canoe tipped, Mack had to rescue them. But while he was doing this, the youngest daughter disappeared.

Ashley had a sinking feeling in her gut as she watched the FBI show up and set up a command centre.

A short time later, Mack was taken by the authorities to a shack up on the nearby mountain. Inside, he positively identified a torn and bloody red dress that had been worn by his daughter on the day of her disappearance. His agonized cry into the night reverberated in Ashley's heart.

Some time later, in winter, Mack found a mysterious note in his mailbox inviting him to spend a weekend at the shack. He went to the post office to ask about the note, still haunted by what had happened to his daughter.

The relationship between Mack and his wife was strained, and she took the kids one weekend to see her brother. There was still love between them, though, and the wife didn't want to lose Mack in addition to their daughter.

This depiction of love made tears form under Ashley's eyelids.

Mack went on a fishing trip up to the mountain, his only companion the painful memories of what had gone so terribly wrong the previous summer.

When he got to the shack, he lay down next to the dried remnants of his daughter's blood, angry at the person who had killed her. Here, he took out a gun and prepared to shoot himself. The only thing that stopped him was a deer who came by the shack at just the right moment.

Leaving the shack, Mack tore up the note, disappointed with God for not showing up.

Ashley found the next part of the movie somewhat confusing. Suddenly it was summertime again, and Mack went into the shack to find three people: a nurturing black woman named Elousia, her Jewish son Yeshua, and an Asian woman named Sarayu. All three claimed to be God.

It was a lot to take in.

As the story played out, Mack had a confrontation with Elousia about his perceptions of God. He accused her of not being around when he needed help. He accused her of not being there for Yeshua, either, when he'd died on the cross.

Elousia softly whispered that Yeshua's death had cost her dearly.

By the time Ashley finished watching the movie, she felt exhausted. But before she went to sleep that night, Ashley got very raw and honest with God.

"I don't know you well at all, but I'm ready to," she prayed. "I'm feeling very lost, very broken and afraid. I don't know how to love you, others, or myself. I feel great anger towards those who have hurt, abused, judged, and misunderstood me, especially those who should have known better! All the same, I'm tired of trying to figure out who I am and what to do. I don't want to venture into new territory, but it's too painful to stay where I am, stuck in the past. I've had enough of living that way. Yeshua, I want the new life you died for me to have. My desire is to get to know who you are afresh, as if we were meeting for the first time. If I find you to be trustworthy, I'll go all-in and follow you anywhere. I'll make you the number one pursuit of my life."

As Ashley got ready for bed, she felt a glimmer of hope in her heart. It was the first time she had felt this way in years.

TWENTY

The next day, Tina invited Ashley to join her and some friends on a bike ride along a trail through the forest. The small group included Ethan, Trent, Mandy, and Arden, and they were going to bring along a picnic lunch.

After thinking about it for a moment, Ashley said yes; she and Tina had always loved going out into the bush.

After meeting up, but before setting out, the friends prayed together, thanking God for his goodness, grace, and mercy. They expressed gratitude for the joy of being united with Yeshua through the power of his Spirit. In awe, they wondered at God's presence everywhere in nature and thanked him for knowing them each fully.

They distributed lunch supplies into each of their backpacks and then began to pedal down the trail. It was a beautiful midsummer day and the breeze blew through the trees. The clear blue sky brought such joy to Ashley's heart. The birds sang high above their heads. She marvelled at the sights, sounds, and smells of creation.

From the front, Tina called to the riders behind her.

"I'd like us each to discover for ourselves part of God's character through nature," she said. "Let's ask ourselves, 'What's one way I can see of his goodness, love, and power today?'"

The trail took them to a river which was spilling out over some rocks. As she watched the waterfall, it seemed to Ashley as though the Holy Spirit was opening her heart to learning more about who God really was.

At one point, the group stopped by a huge rocky hill. Trent wanted to climb to the top to find out what was up there. He was always eager for an adventure—and after some discussion, it turned out that Arden, Mandy, Tina, and Ethan were all game.

Ashley heard the soft whisper in her heart: *"Take a step out, no matter what size, to trust me. You will encounter me along the way."*

They locked up their bikes against some trees off the trail and began to climb. Along the way, they encountered a side trail made by some rabbit and deer. Some continued up the main trail while others took the diversion.

The trails ended up coming together again at the top of the hill, where the view was breathtaking. In the distance, over a great expanse of forest, they saw the remains of an old mining town. That was their eventual destination.

Before they could continue, though, the skies suddenly opened up and rain began to fall. In short order, a full-blown storm descended on them.

The group hurried back down to the bottom of hill, grabbing their bikes and praying for help from God to find shelter.

Ashley felt herself panicking a little. Tina instinctively picked up on this.

"It's okay, Ashley," Tina assured her. "You can trust that God will take care of us. He loves us and looks after those who delight in him. The Bible invites us to drink deeply of the pleasures of God. We experience for ourselves the joyous mercies he gives to all who turn to hide themselves in him."

Just as Tina said this, Father Light blanketed the group with his peace and tangible presence.

About ten minutes later, they came to a fork in the trail—a smaller path diverged to the left, along with a sign that suggested a trapper's cabin in that direction.

"Let's check it out!" shouted Ethan over the sound of the rain.

A minute later, they entered a clearing around a log cabin. They parked their bikes against the neighbouring woodshed, then found shelter under the cabin's covered porch. Ashley let out a shriek of surprise when she looked down and discovered a pool of dried blood on the wooden floorboards.

Trent, Ethan, and Arden entered the cabin first, and inside they found a middle-aged man with a broken leg lying on one of several bunks. He wore a white undershirt, having hung up his plaid shirt at the end of the bed. The musty cabin smelled like sweat.

Trent suddenly understood the reason for the sudden storm.

"Sir, my name is Trent," he said to the man, speaking with compassion. "My friends and I came to wait out the storm, but we'd like to help you."

"Well, I'll be darned! I'm Jackson and I busted up my leg pretty good night before last on the trail. Was able to hobble in here and make myself a temporary splint. But gosh darn it, I forgot my satellite phone in the truck. Last night, I was frantically wondering how to get out of here. So I called out to God, asking if someone might help me out of this jam. I grew up in these woods and ain't used to relying on no one but myself. But ya'll showing up like this... well, it makes me wonder if someone was listening."

Arden pulled up a rickety wooden chair and sat down. "You betcha someone was listening! Over lunch, we can share stories about our Creator listening when we call. We brought food with us and are willing to share. We'll use one of our phones to call in an air ambulance."

Ethan went back outside to update the women on the situation.

"Come on, let's grab some firewood from that shed," he said after explaining about the man. "We need to start a fire."

Soon Ethan and the women walked inside, their arms full of chopped wood.

"Well, ain't you three ladies a sight for sore eyes!" Jackson exclaimed. "If you boys need to head on out, leave ya phone and these pretty little things can take care of all my needs! Bet they're the reason you seem to be glowing!"

Tina recoiled as he eyed them like big pieces of meat. "Jackson, we don't appreciate your implication. We're not merely objects to be used for personal pleasure. Our lives have enormous value, just like yours. We've been made to be honoured and protected, not abused and used!"

Jackson went red in the face with sheepishness. Or maybe it was anger. Yet a spark of respect came into his eyes.

"I'm sorry, lass," he said. "Won't you come in and have a sit down?"

Tina shook her head. "No thank you. We'll go sit outside on the porch and have lunch."

Before heading out, the women put down the firewood next to the fireplace.

"I'll join you," Ethan said to the women.

Arden took out his phone. "And I'll call for that air ambulance."

As Arden dialled, Ethan stepped outside, where Tina, Ashley, and Mandy had started getting out the food.

"Are you ladies okay?" he asked.

"I'm so very tired of that kind of unwanted male attention," Tina said. "And I hate when people only value me for being small and attractive. I know that we're called to forgive and not hold on to offences, but that doesn't mean we had to stay in that situation."

"Well said," Mandy agreed. "Thank you for standing up for us. You only barely beat me to it. You're right, though. We've just got to let it go."

Ashley watched them in amazement. Had her sister just stood up to a bully? She'd never seen anything like that while growing up with her. Tina had always been more likely to run and hide in the pages a book. Now she sensed courage and confidence.

"What's happened to you in the years since we were children?" Ashley asked when they were alone.

"What you're seeing, Ashley, is the evidence that I'm getting my acceptance from God rather than people," Tina told her. "A person can't take away what they never gave me. God accepts me, and that was made possible by what Yeshua did by dying in our place and rising again. Now I put my trust in his finished work. He's unlocked my heart and made me into a new woman. I'm still learning about what it means to be a new creation by faith in Yeshua Christ, but it all comes from walking it out with the Holy Trio in personal relationship."

This gave Ashley a lot to think about. She recognized that her sister had changed, and this was proof of God's goodness.

To give herself a little space, Ashley walked over to Ethan. "Do you have any sandwiches and snacks in your backpack?" she asked.

"Sure. I've got about a third of the lunch supplies, but I can go back inside for the rest."

When Ethan walked in again, he saw Trent bent over the fireplace, trying to start a fire. He was in the middle of a deep conversation with Jackson.

"She's right, you know," Trent was saying. "As men, we were made to live with honour and courage, upholding the value of life and protecting it. I've seen firsthand the pain women go through. My own sister was abused by her ex—physically, emotionally, and verbally—when I was twenty. I froze at the time, not knowing what to do. But I knew it wasn't right. As I matured and became a man through right relationship with God, my perspective changed. I began to understand that the world we live in isn't as the Creator intended. It's upside-down compared to how we were made to live. We all have deep long-ings that give us a glimpse of the world we were supposed to live in. Desires for courage, honour, respect, and legacy. Hope, joy, love, laughter, and safety. We were created to build our lives on stable, life-giving relationships."

At this point, Arden hung up the phone and walked back over to them. "The air ambulance will be here in forty-five min-utes to an hour."

Jackson nodded, looking relieved by this piece of good news.

Arden sat in the rickety chair and leaned forward. He felt a prompting in his heart to ask a specific question.

"Who do you think God is, Jackson?" Arden said.

"To be honest, I thought I was my own god. But honestly, I'm very broken. I try and look like I have everything together, but I don't."

Arden sighed. "I don't have everything together either. None of us do. Nor do we have to. But we constantly rely on God's grace and mercy. Mercy is when we don't get what we deserve, and grace is when we receive what we don't deserve. We all deserve punishment in this life, and the next, for everything we've done wrong. But because of God's great love, his Son Yeshua took the punishment for us, even though he had done no wrong. He was the only perfect man who ever lived. In faith, and in the power of his Father, he died in our place. The Holy Spirit then raised Yeshua from the dead on the third day. None of us deserves forgiveness from God, but he freely gives it when we repent and put our trust in Yeshua Christ. In him, we come alive in every area where we were once dead."

Ethan was quietly observing all this as he felt a prompting from the Holy Spirit. He picked up the remaining backpacks of food and returned outside to the porch.

He felt certain that the Lord wanted to do something.

"I sense that the Holy Spirit wants to so or speak something very specific," he said to the women, who were already in the process of unpacking lunch. "Let's just be still in our hearts and listen."

"What do I do?" Ashley asked.

Tina took her hand gently. "Just ask the Holy Spirit what he's trying to say. Where is Father Light's heart in this situation? Then just be quiet and listen. Sometimes I close my eyes to help me focus."

The three sat in silence for the next several minutes.

Right away, Tina heard the Holy Spirit speak to her heart about the situation. He spoke in pure love, truth, and conviction.

"Jackson is my son, too. He's also worth the blood of Yeshua. We gave up so much for him to have the choice to know us as we are. To come home and be remade as he was. We call our children to love not because of what they do, but because it's who they are in relationship with us. Those who struggle to believe in us need tangible proof that our love can powerfully transform them."

Ashley heard this, too, and could relate. In her own life, she could see the consequences of not always seeing evidence of God in the lives of people around her.

"Yeshua died so that you would be completely free," the voice said to Ashley. *"Stop getting offended. Stop living in the past."*

Tina pressed her eyes closed even harder as the Holy Spirit continued to share his heart with her.

"I want you to share the reality of forgiveness with Jackson. Show him our messy grace. Remember, Yeshua taught you to forgive because of how much you have been forgiven. He forgives and cleanses you daily when you turn your heart back towards him. It's an integral part of our journey together."

Tina opened her eyes and looked one by one at the others on the porch. "The Holy Spirit is prompting me to go back inside and do something," she said. "Stay here and only come in when you sense the Lord leading you to do so."

Getting up, Tina took a deep breath and reminded herself of the price that had been paid for her life. She also remembered the extravagant love of the Holy Trio.

When she was ready, she took a step and opened the door of the cabin.

Inside, she found Arden and Trent sitting in chairs around the bunk where Jackson lay. The fire was burning in the hearth and the temperature was beginning to rise.

Sensing that the time was right, Tina dove right in.

"Jackson, your comment about women did make me angry," she began. "It has the potential to hurt me... but only if I let it. So I forgive you for that and choose to let it go. I won't hold it against you, for I too have been forgiven much. I'm not perfect, so I shouldn't expect perfection from others."

She paused for a moment, took another deep breath, and kept going.

"Honestly, walking with God as a Christian isn't always rosy and easy. It's about having an ongoing relationship with the Holy Trio, making them your ultimate passion. It's also about humility. We're each going through the journey of being fashioned in the image of our Creator, allowing them to lead and heal us, receiving what they freely give. We walk that out and refine our character, making us more mature. Yes, we're imperfect and in process, but we don't limit our expectation that God will finish the work he started in our lives through Yeshua. You're worth dying for. You are the Father's son, too. You were also part of the joy set before Yeshua when he endured the cross."

As Tina shared, gradually Jackson became aware of the warmth in the room, and it wasn't just the fire. It was unconditional love, the result of God's power and love falling upon the cabin. He felt completely seen by the source of this warmth, and also completely accepted. It was overwhelming and beautiful; Jackson craved more. The Holy Spirit was all over him, wooing his heart.

The others could also sense the holiness of the moment.

"We honour your presence with and in us, Holy Spirit," said Trent. "Let us all spontaneously share what's on our hearts before God and one another."

Tina pipped in first. "Holy Spirit, thank you for revealing the goodness of God, and for teaching us how to walk in his righteousness. We're so grateful that we get to know you personally as we journey through life with you. You reveal anything that's in our hearts that needs to be removed."

"God, you love us so unconditionally, even though we're a broken and needy people," said Arden. "Your grace and mercies are new every single day. Thank you for the faith-based righteousness that's freely available to all who put their trust and faith in Yeshua. You are so kind. So patient. We're grateful to know you as our Creator and hear your word. Joy overflows in our hearts. You are enough for us, God!"

As everyone shared, the tangible presence of the Holy Spirit in the cabin increased. Love washed over the inhabitants in waves as the Lord changed their perspectives and expressed his heart for them.

In the midst of his presence, Jackson was being reborn of the Spirit.

"God, I want to know you as you are," Jackson said as he turned his heart towards the Creator. "I thought I was my own god, but now I realize that I'm a broken human in need of you. I ask you to save me from myself and make me your own. Please forgive me for all the wrong I've done. I want to come home to be with you."

Trent raised his hands in praise. "Holy Spirit, thank you for making your forever home inside of Jackson."

"Burn up and remove anything in our lives that doesn't belong," said Arden. "Get rid of anything that isn't in line with the Father's heart."

"We belong to you, Yeshua," Trent broke in again. "You are our Saviour and Redeemer, the only way back to fullness and completion and right relationship with the good God who made us. You are so wonderful. You are the God who does the impossible, making all things new."

Mandy walked into the cabin and immediately sensed the tangible presence of the Holy Spirit. She came in and sat down in one of the chairs. As she did, she received a powerful dose of the love of God. The Holy Spirit was refreshing and restoring the hearts and souls of everyone present.

Trent continued with his confident declarations. "Yeshua, you have defeated fear, death, and sin so we could die to that old way of living and be alive to God. We put our trust in you, no matter what happens. Your faithfulness and devotion actively make us new from the inside out, completely set free and redeemed. You are worthy of our worship and praise, our entire lives, because of what you've done."

"There's no longer any room for us to live in the past," Mandy said, adding even more passionate praise. "We have no right to be offended. Yet you're worth it all! You are the one we've been searching and longing for our whole lives. We refuse to let you go now that we've been found by you. Now that we know why we were made, we refuse to walk away."

At times, no one said anything. There was no need, for the Holy Spirit was there, loving each one of them, making them more complete like Yeshua. He refreshed them, changed their mindsets, and spoke what was on the Father's heart. He did a beautiful and unique work in each person's life, because no two of them were exactly alike. Each were made to relate to God in different way.

This was the atmosphere when Ethan and Ashley walked in. They simply joined in, continuing to be as focused on the Holy Spirit as they had been outside.

It was a wonderful experience as the whole group luxuriated in the love of God, in turn loving this triune being. The Holy Trio was a wondrous mystery and not one of them had the desire to leave or interrupt what the Spirit was doing. His perfect love cast out every fear as Yeshua cast out lies. The glory of God was evident in that cabin, and none of its occupants could express in words the full impact of encountering the presence of God so tangibly.

When the air ambulance came, the paramedics noticed the peaceful atmosphere in the cabin. Taken aback, they couldn't help but wonder what was going on. None of them could leave, though, without the patient.

As effectively as they could, the team loaded Jackson into the helicopter. One of them also took Arden's number in case there were any critical developments while en route to the hospital.

Even as the helicopter took off, Jackson kept sharing with the paramedics what the goodness of God's pure love had done for him and how Yeshua had changed his life. His new faith was founded on the power of God, just as God had intended it to be from the beginning.

EPILOGUE

After the air ambulance had taken Jackson to the hospital in Thunder Bay, the friends sat around the cabin joking and laughing. Tina suggested they go around and share what they saw in each other of God's heart and nature. The point was to honour God's image in them.

Trent spoke first.

"Mandy, you have such a nurturing heart," he said. "You desire and actively seek more in the life we were made for. You genuinely love and care for people, carrying a compassion for those who are hurting. You aren't afraid to take risks and try new things. You're such a precious treasure, a woman of great worth who takes the time to mature in the Lord. You have a deep beauty that comes from the Lord. You shine brightest in your times of intimacy with our creative Holy Trio."

"Ashley, you are an amazing and precious treasure," Tina said next as she turned to her sister. "You're unafraid to ask hard questions of yourself and others. You desire authentic and deep relationships. Your soul is thirsty for more. You were crafted by Father Light with a unique and beautiful design, inside and out. You have a wonderful gift of creativity. You're willing to go the extra mile and step out of the familiar in search of answers.

I encourage you to take your needs of love, acceptance, and acknowledgement to God. Allow him to fill, heal, and complete you in a way nothing else could. I love you, my dear sister!"

Filled with love for God and her sister, Ashley went next.

"Tina, you have the heart of a worshipper and warrior. Your strength stems from your strong faith in God. You trust our Creator and take the Holy Trio at their word. Your words are powerful because you speak words of life, empowered by the Holy Spirit. You dare to leave the past behind and go all-in for God, passionately devoting your life to him. You're willing to humble yourself when you make a mistake. When you share your heart, it's precious. You love to dance and laugh. And if you slip up, you're willing to get back up and accept a helping hand."

There was a moment of silence before Mandy spoke.

"Trent, in you I see the Father's heart to love, nurture, care, and protect. You have a loyalty in friendship and a desire to live intentionally. You also have an adventurous spirit to explore and discover things. You ask questions and have a curious nature, desiring to serve in love by helping to build up the body as you're empowered through relationship with the Holy Spirit. You have a gift of leadership that calls out the best of God in others and challenges them to arise. The Lord has given you eyes to see others, even strangers, as Father Light sees them."

Ethan looked across the room at his friend Arden, who he so appreciated.

"Arden, in your life I see a vitality and zest," Ethan shared. "You have a passion for God and the well-being of his family. You look for small ways to honour your brothers and sisters. You and Trent also love to have fun, and you're comfortable in your own skin. This means you're game to try weird and random things. You hunger for more of God and intentionally seek him. You also have a creative and adventurous streak. You really listen to people and want authentic relationships. You have the courage and inner strength, like that of a tiger."

Smiling, Arden turned towards Ethan. "And you, my friend, have a strong passion for God and the simple power of the gospel. I respect how you seek to honour others in everything and draw them out in conversation. You're filled to overflowing with the joy of the Lord, intentionally building on God and the power of his word. You humbly allow the Holy Spirit to lead and teach you in everything, living as a man of integrity through relationship with our Creator. You also ask questions and are willing to talk through differences in discussion with other believers. You invite men of quality, honour, and strong faith to speak into your life."

The group remained there for a long time, lingering and enjoying one another's company. They knew they were incomplete without God and each other as part of a team. Through eyes of faith, they saw the beauty all around them—and they loved one another because God had first loved them. They knew the worth placed on their lives through the sacrifice of Yeshua Christ.

They took communion together using crackers and grape juice in order to remember what Yeshua had done for them, for the whole world, so all would know the love and goodness of God through choosing to be in right relationship with him. He would do anything to reveal how much humans desperately needed to know him, and to realize that the point of life was to be known as they truly were.

"We are stronger together with our Creator God and one another," said Tina as they finished their time of communion. "He calls us by name and invites us into an adventurous life with him. How we choose to respond is up to each of us…"

The Holy Trio—Father Light, Yeshua, and the Holy Spirit—delighted in listening to this conversation as the friends shared their power and love as it actively worked in their lives. It was a joy to watch them laugh, cry, and pray for one another, building up one another with the gifts of grace they had each been given.

ABOUT THE AUTHOR

Grace E.M. Allan is the pseudonym for a woman who lives in Northwestern Ontario. She is an artist, writer, storyteller, photographer, missionary, volunteer, adventurer, and teacher focusing on connection with God. She encounters His presence through Bible reading, prayer, worship, surrender, creativity, fellowship, discipleship, sermons, quietness (Psalm 46:10), humility, and music in her daily life. She has followed God's voice into Youth with a Mission, nonprofit work, and being creative with God. She is inspired by testimonies, books, conversations, sunsets, playing games, reading, nature, worship, fellowship, and hikes.

Grace has experienced God's love, which draws, works, melts, heals, restores, frees, purifies, and transforms along life's journey. Her desire is to share a story that reveals the goodness of God through Jesus, aka Yeshua in Hebrew.

She lives and works in Northern Ontario, has a home-based studio, and was connected, for a time, with the Created to Thrive Mentoring Group. She has volunteered with kids ministry through camps, leading, and teaching for several years.

To be honest, none of Grace's life's experiences fully qualify her to write a novel on loving one's mortal enemies, the supernatural realm, or the miraculous working power of God. But as Paul wrote, paraphrased, "I count all of these as a loss that I might gain Christ." He is the qualifier for this book and the reason why it is in print.

Grace did not hear, see, or believe anything of God's miraculous power until she was twenty-two years old. She focused more on doubting God than believing in him and faced multiple family situations that appeared insurmountable. But God, in mercy, love, tenderness, patience, kindness, and redemption, began to do a new unexpected thing in her life.

May your faith be built up while reading that nothing is impossible for God, and that while we were enemies of God, Christ died for us. May your entire being yearn more for the essence of God in your life.